P9-BZB-294

JUST UNDER THE CLOUDS

JUST UNDER THE CLOUDS

MELISSA SARNO

Alfred A. Knopf
New York

THIS IS A BORZOI BOOK PUBLISHED BY ALFRED A. KNOPF

All rights reserved. Published in the United States by Alfred A. Knopf, an imprint of Random House Children's Books, a division of Penguin Random House LLC, New York.

Knopf, Borzoi Books, and the colophon are registered trademarks of Penguin Random House LLC.

Visit us on the Web! rhcbooks.com

Educators and librarians, for a variety of teaching tools, visit us at RHTeachersLibrarians.com

Library of Congress Cataloging-in-Publication Data
is available upon request.
ISBN 978-1-5247-2008-7 (trade) — ISBN 978-1-5247-2009-4 (lib. bdg.) — ISBN 978-1-5247-2010-0 (ebook)

Interior design by Jaclyn Whalen

The text of this book is set in 12.25-point Horley Old Style MT.

Printed in the United States of America
June 2018
10 9 8 7 6 5 4 3 2 1

First Edition

For Tyler,
my home

Just Under the Clouds

Chapter 1

Mom's calling and I'm counting. My backpack's tight on my back up here in the tree. Knees tucked neat over the branches. Bare feet dangling. *One . . . two . . . three . . .* I soar. Out and then down and I'm at the dirt, balancing on the tree's roots, while Adare spreads out on a clump of Brooklyn brown grass, like a snow angel without the snow.

"Coming!" I shout. I scoop up Adare's hand. "Come on, you."

Her breath is caught. She's got a habit of holding it.

"Adare." I stomp.

But her eyes are wide and they shine like gray glass. The sun's in them, all pretty, sparkling, the way light hits water.

"Adare!" I close my eyes and wish her breath free.

She lets go of it and squirms her hand out of mine, then

takes off running toward Mom, who'll take us from the park back to Ennis House.

We've never lived in a shelter before, and even if we've never lived much of anywhere for too long, it feels like, for the first time, we don't have a home. We're *homeless*. For real.

"Cora, I thought I told you to quit climbing. You've got to keep an eye on your sister after school," Mom scolds as I chase behind.

Adare is buried in the limp of Mom's shirt.

"I did," I argue, but I know it's no use. I take Mom's hand in mine. It always feels like I've got to remind her I'm here, too. Her hands are pink and stained.

"Why are they pink?" I ask.

She smiles. "You'll see." Then she leans down so her whisper's at my messy hair. "What do we have today?"

I open up my own hand. "A butterfly."

She squeezes it tight because we might not have a ton of money or clothes, but now we have a monarch butterfly I drew in blue ink. Right there on my palm.

We walk the sidewalks to Ennis House. Adare and I march on opposite sides of Mom.

I call out trees as we pass. Pin oak. Honey locust. Linden. Maple. The female ginkgo drops berries that smell awful. I gave that one a name a long time ago. It's called the vomit tree. When you pass one, you'd better hold your nose.

"What's that?" Mom asks, pointing at a piney-looking tree.

I reach up and run its prickle over my thumb to count how many needles are bunched together on each branch. "White pine," I say fast.

She shakes her head in surprise. "How can you tell?"

"Five needles per bundle." I grin while she squeezes my hand again. She knows I've studied the photographs Daddy pasted in his field journal, which I call my Tree Book. She knows I've got my eye out for all the plants and trees I can find.

Like always, Adare stops a few thousand times during our ten-minute walk. She looks toward the sky, her chin sailing up like a flyaway balloon. I keep my sighs secret. Loud enough in my head so only I can hear them. We're getting nowhere fast, and even if everything in me is itching to complain, I don't say a word.

Adare was born special, Mom always says. She tells the story like it's legend. She talks about the wind that night, in its quickening swirl. She talks about the labor, long and uneasy, Adare turning circles in her womb. She talks about the moment Adare came into the world without a sound— *Not blue, no, more like lavender, like sunset*—and in that moment all the oxygen gone from the world, the trees forgetting to breathe their gift, Adare forgetting, too.

She lost oxygen to the brain, but Mom doesn't call it a disadvantage, like others do. *Adare sees things a different way,* she always says. *It's like all of us see from here*—she places her hand at the level of her heart. *And Adare sees from up here*—she sends her arm soaring.

Up where? That's what I always wonder.

We stop at the corner. In the distance the big cranes dangle a bunch of car parts. The scrap metal piles are like rolling hills just past the BQE. We live near the canal now and I like it. The water might smell of dirt and weeds and rot, but when you stare at it real close, there's a looping oil swirl and it looks like a broken rainbow nobody sees.

Inside Ennis House, the stairwell lights are burned out and the glass is split. Old Lou hovers, his eyes like two brown beetles, as Mom pushes us past.

"Don't linger," she says. We walk the dirty floor, past the smack of cockroach, which has been there three days. I've counted.

Mom's hand stiffens, then tightens, like it always does. She squeezes my butterfly palm flat and everything in me knows better than to complain.

As we climb up the stairs, Mrs. Johnson shouts from behind the door with a voice that stomps the air and Fred C.'s place smells like sweet onions and old grill. My stomach starts roaring and in my head I tell it to quiet down. But it doesn't listen.

When we get to five, my legs are burning and my sunflower backpack feels so heavy, it's like it's full of sinking rocks. Mom holds Adare's backpack for her—the one I picked out for her at Winn Discount. I made sure it was bright blue like the sky.

The hall's dark and narrow and we file through, Mom's hand still crushing mine.

"It smells like cat pee."

"It's a trick," Mom says. "To keep the mice away."

Mom says you can buy all you want at places like Miss Li's grocery. She says it's called predator pee.

But we've got our own cat, Sookie, even if she's more Adare's than mine, sticking like glue to her and hissing at me. Mom jiggles the keys and opens the lock. Sookie takes one look at me and skitters underneath the quilt, which only draws attention to our messy mattress on the floor.

Mom shakes her head, guides us in, and deadbolts the door. "I thought I told you to make the bed."

"What's the sense in making a bed when you're just going to get right back in?"

Mom gives a *Don't get smart with me* kind of look and I run around the mattress, pulling the sheets real fast, so they flutter-puff up and settle down. That always cracks Adare up, so I fluff them high again, and she's got this sniffy laugh that always makes Mom smile.

Adare throws herself on the settling sheets. Her laughs are trampled and caught. I pull up the candy-colored quilt over her, quick. I love how soft it is from years of washing. Then I sit gently on her bony legs, pretending she's not even there.

I announce it real loud: "Bed's made!" Adare laughs and squirms, and Mom plays along, too.

She says, "Cora, I can't find Adare. Do you know where she is?" until Adare is wriggling and laughing and poking her head out, her hair falling over her eyes in a tangle. It makes me smile when she smiles, sweet and pink.

Her voice is soft, like always, even if she sounds less like she's ten and more like a baby. "I'm right here."

"You're right here," I say.

"Yeah."

Then she runs for her butterfly wings, slips them over her shoulders, and heads to the open window. She sits next to the broken screen and sets out peanuts on the ledge. She rests her elbows and waits for her family of crows.

"Adare, stop that," Mom scolds.

Mom doesn't know what we know, that at our old place on Hoyt Street they came and left Adare gifts. She got a silver screw, a button, and a crooked earring, which she keeps in an old tea box on the sill. We're wondering when the crows at Ennis House will start leaving things, too.

I notice the curtains are different and I point. "They're pink," I marvel.

"This morning's project."

When Mom gets bored with a place, she starts in on art projects. But no matter how many ways she tries to make the space look like home, she's never satisfied.

She holds up her stained hands. "I dyed them with beet juice. Isn't that amazing?"

I groan. "No more beets." We've been eating them for days, from boxes at the Red Hook farm. They've turned my pee a watercolor-pink swirl.

"They're beautiful," Mom says. "Little purple moons."

A violet puddle sits beneath the dripping curtains in the shape of a lopsided heart.

For six years since Daddy died, we've been making homes where we can get them, from place to place. Sometimes we cuddle up on Mom's artist friends' couches. Once we rode back and forth on the 4 train all night long, looking at the fluorescent lights like they were stars.

Until a few months ago, we stayed the longest we ever stayed anywhere. Even if it was only one room on Hoyt Street in Carroll Gardens, it was ours, and sun poured in and Mom painted murals on the walls and I loved it so much I thought it'd be a forever home. Until one day Mom sat me down and said, *We can't keep up. Not every month.* When I asked, *Keep what up?* she said, *Rent,* and it felt like before she could say anything else, we were tossed out with only our blankets and the things that matter, like my Tree Book and Adare's butterfly wings, which she's worn dirt-thin.

That's how we ended up here at Ennis House.

We're on a list, waiting for housing we can afford for

real this time. Mom says we move up the list, like it's a ladder. She turns her papers in on time, marches up all the right steps, knocks on all the right doors, and we're waiting, as she says, *for word*. But it never seems to come. Our caseworker, Tilda, tells us over and over, like we need reminding, *You're not a bum. You don't stink. This is not forever.* All I can think is: If it's not forever, does it have to be now?

"How're your seeds doing?" Mom asks, pouring water from the kettle for tea, a habit of Daddy's she can't let go of.

She watches it sit and steam. When it's ready, she motions the sign of the cross, in his memory. Forehead, heart, and shoulders. She closes her eyes and takes her first sip. I hope it matters. I hope the love finds its way to heaven. To him.

I turn my attention to the windowsill, where my greenhouse sits. We've made a lot of greenhouses over the years and this is one of the best. It's made into a cube of old windowpanes and the roof latches with fasteners Mom nailed down.

I open them, careful, like a present where the wrapping's so nice, it almost doesn't matter what's inside. My seeds are in tiny rows and I can't wait to harvest the spinach and the lettuce when the leaves sprout up. We haven't had much luck growing things in the past. Either the seeds stay hidden or we get one crooked green line shoot up and fall limp.

But it's March now and this spring is a first. This spring we've got all kinds of somethings sprouting and two small leaves from each stalk. They're like the wings of a bird, the way little kids draw them sometimes. A bird that looks like the letter V. "Leaves."

"*True* leaves," Mom reminds me, the way Daddy used to.

"True leaves," I repeat.

True leaves are what you call the first leaves up. Like we can't believe them until they sprout. Like until then it's all been a lie. But I know you can only grow things if you have faith in them from the very beginning.

Chapter 2

That night, I can't sleep. I'm holding in my pee because it's too cold to go out in the hall and I don't want to wake up Mom and we're not allowed to leave without her because of Old Lou. We've got a bucket for emergencies, but it freaks me out—the idea of collecting it like that. It makes me think Miss Li will bottle it up and sell it like the predator pee.

Sookie is at our feet and I try and curl my toes up into her belly, measuring the in and out of her breath. I listen to the steady rush of the highway and squeeze my legs tight. Just not too tight or I'll explode.

I lean in close to Adare. I listen for Mom, curled up underneath the mohair blanket in the pink beanbag chair. Adare and I, we're the exact same size, even if I'm twelve and she's only ten. Our eyes are like Mom's. *A kicked-up-dust brown,* she calls them. And I say they're mixed with gray storm clouds. We've got the same skin, a little tan and freckled, and the same skinny arms, all dangly and long.

People say we'd be twins if it wasn't for our hair. Mine's a messy honey-colored thing, all tangled. Adare's is auburn, especially in the sun, and it runs down her back like silk. Mom says that's from our daddy's red hair. That was the Irish in him. So the Irish in us is all in Adare.

The rest of us is all Mom and the Mexican Americans in South Texas. Daddy called her his rose, like the song, his *Rose of San Antone.* When people ask why she doesn't speak Spanish, she says her family's more American than the Pilgrims. *They moved a border,* she says, drawing a line in the air, *and we've been American ever since.* When people ask me why I don't speak Spanish, I say I speak Brooklyn.

People say Adare and I could be twins, but what they really mean is, we'd be twins if Adare could speak right, if she knew how to read and write, if she didn't have to go to special classes or get so excited about a red balloon or the sparkle in someone's necklace that her breath speeds up like a set of wheezing drums.

When Adare sleeps next to me, I like to match up our palms. I like to make our toes touch. I like it that underneath the old quilt that's nearly lost its stitch we're two noodles, stuck together. That in the dark, with Adare asleep and me dreaming awake, we're one and the same.

I squeeze my legs tight. Sookie's fur is soft at my toes.

Outside, the streetlamp is orange and it shines up the

tree bark. It's a London plane tree, but I call it a patch tree because the bark is peeling all over in yellows and browns and greens. There are six on this street. In my Tree Book I mark down all the trees around all the homes we've ever lived in.

I remember that I didn't mark down the white pine on the way from school to here. So I reach under my pillow and pull out my Tree Book.

The worn brown leather is cold in my hands and I fumble in the dark, slipping out the turquoise ribbon, which keeps my place. Daddy used the book for field notes when he worked in gardens in Gowanus, and Mom gave it to me a few days after he died. She placed it in my hands and told me it held on to the secret of all the growing things.

His notes are in fine print on the lined pages. All numbers. Measurements and temperatures. Rainfall and sun. There are charts on soil moisture. Inches. Dates. I try to read it, like code. I want more than anything to understand his chicken-scratch writing. But all I've got is numbers, and numbers are not what I'm good at.

White pine, I write in the dark. I add it to my tree map of Ennis House. For a minute, I think of giving it a name—like I gave the vomit tree a name—but *white pine* sounds just fine.

Daddy labeled his pages with Latin names and photographs. Like *Ailanthus altissima,* the last thing he studied.

He told Mom it was his favorite tree because it can grow in the worst conditions. It can grow anywhere. I looked it up in a reference book at the school library and it's got a nonscientific name, too: tree of heaven.

I turn to the first page of Daddy's tree of heaven notes. A photograph. Then he tracks the tree, page after page, in charts. Every day for months and months until the numbers fall off and slip away.

The last page was written the day he died and now it's worn and loose and hanging on to the notebook by a thread. It's labeled *Ailanthus altissima, March 21*. There's one note on temperature in his scratchy scrawl.

It's the last thing I have from the person he used to be.

Daddy always said a tree has a vascular system, just like a person. It transfers water and food like blood. If a tree doesn't die of some catastrophe, it can rot away, like a disease to the heart that no one knows is coming. In Daddy's case, he died because his heart grew too big—so big, it couldn't pump blood and it lost all its rhythm. It doesn't seem fair for anyone to die of a too-big heart, but he was gone before anyone could even try to get it beating right again.

I look out the window. If you can get into a tree around here, you can see far away, over the green ick of the canal, and there are all these little water towers like tiny stilt houses on top of houses. I've always thought that if we could each have one little tower, me and Adare and Mom, right next to each other, we could make up our own spaces just the way we want them.

I close my eyes and dream our towers. An open-roof tower for Adare so she can look straight to the sky for her crows. Blank canvas walls for Mom to paint the way she used to before she had to spend all her time making money at the store. Mine, all glass, with yellow light flooding in, so I can grow things everywhere. I'd have my own sink and toilet and a toothbrush holder like we used to have on Hoyt Street, the kind where your toothbrush dangles like it's sitting in its own little inner tube.

Sookie does this sigh thing where her belly puffs out into a mini hot-air balloon, and before I know it, my belly's the opposite, empty and soft, and the dream of my tower is warm and sweet, and I feel like I'm floating until I realize what I've done.

I push the blankets and gut-punch Sookie with my heel without meaning to. She does this hiss-whimper thing and Adare moans and my underwear's soaked right through to the faded flower sheet. Twelve years old and I peed myself like a little kid.

I can't believe it. I've always been able to hold it. I sit up and wriggle my underpants to my ankles so I'm in only my lace tank top. I leave them there, with Sookie prowling underneath the covers. Adare rolls over, closer to the big old wet beet-pee stain. I can see she's awake, her eyes like two shining stars in the dark. She rubs them until she's up and sitting and I see her mouth slide down into a frown. I shush her real fast.

"You're dreaming," I say.

But I wish it was me who was. I could crumple the sheets, burn them with a match I don't have. I could say I spilled my tea after our boxed macaroni-and-cheese dinner and I think of running to get a mug real quick. But they're stacked in the drying rack. Mom cleared it all before bed.

Adare hates being woken up. She starts this steady yelping pout and I try to shush her again, but I hear Mom rustle on the beanbag chair. She murmurs, "Adare?"

Then, before I know what I'm doing, I yank at Adare's polka-dot underwear. She squirms and cries out. I wrestle the underwear to her feet and jump out of bed. My bare toes hit the cold wood floor and I rush to the dresser, rummaging in the dark through socks and shirts. "It's okay," I call out to Mom and Adare. I wrangle my legs into a soft, clean pair.

Adare's crying real tears now and Mom's awake and fumbling for the light-bulb string dangling in the middle of the room.

The light is an angry blast. I hold up Adare's polka-dot underwear in the air and call out, "I have a clean pair for you."

Mom's eyes are hazy. She looks around, adjusting to the light.

"She peed herself," I whisper.

The lie is at my stomach, sitting there sick and hunched.

Mom goes to Adare and wraps her up in the cloak of her arms, and I know if it was me, she wouldn't be so kind. "It was an accident," she assures her.

And Adare is as she always is, falling into our embraces, trusting that she is who we say.

Chapter 3

The next morning, I walk into Mrs. Belz's class, still thinking about the accident, how we stripped the sheets, washed my skivvies in dish soap, and hung them to dry.

Meredith Crane watches me with a stink in her eye. She already thinks everything I do is *babyish*. She's always watching me as I drag Adare around after school, climb trees, and carry a giant backpack instead of a shoulder bag. She makes fun of me when I braid my messy hair or make fortune-tellers out of notebook paper. It's like she can see straight through to the wrong underwear and know I'm the baby who wet the bed.

I slip my backpack from my arm, slump into my cold blue metal seat. I used to talk to kids, but with the way we keep getting yanked around Brooklyn, tossed out like useless weeds, I keep my mouth shut. What would be the point?

Mrs. Belz's class is about as strict and boring as it gets. It's not like my art class, where you can talk and laugh and work on anything that puts you in a *creative frenzy*, as Mrs. Folaris likes to say. Mrs. Belz is already slapping her chalk against the board, thwacking it like hail pellets. She draws long formulas, looped in parentheses, with a's and b's squared and plus-signed and looking rude.

The bell rings, fast and shrill. Sabina Griffin's annoying rubber boots screech across the floor like always and Mrs. Belz is all *Settle down, settle down.* The chairs scratch the tiles, Meredith Crane fiddles with a pink eraser at her desk, and I'm bored already, so I let my eyes wander to the window to keep track.

There's one patch tree past the courtyard and there's a cherry blossom, short and bushy, its branches sticking out in a perfect oval. It's budding early this year and the sun cuts across it, slicing it in half.

I reach down to my backpack and pull out my Tree Book. I smooth out the soft pages and write in quick pencil scratch: *Cherry blossom. Buds. Mid-March.* In addition to making tree maps, I mark all the beginnings and endings of a thing growing. I write tiny, using every available inch of blank space. I never want the pages to run out.

I look out the window, like I do every day from this seat, studying the rows of trees.

I mark them in code. The Callery pears are pear-shaped. The honey locusts are like fat, squat bears. And the pin oaks stand in skinny, straight lines.

To anyone else my map probably looks like a jumble of pencil scratches, but to me it's a walking path. There's an order to it. It follows my feet to all the places we've ever lived. I scrape the sidewalks, look up, then send the life of the city back down to the pages. It holds on to me. It keeps me. And I need a way of staying.

I glance at Mrs. Belz. She looks pleased that I'm taking notes.

Before I got to middle school, math was easy, but now I try to make sense of every number and letter, how they're all arranged. I don't understand why there's a number *after* the equal sign and why we don't need an answer but the missing piece of a question instead. Mom says when it clicks, it clicks, and I keep waiting for that moment. But it just doesn't come.

I go through class this way, from the window to the board, mixing tree and sky and the way the clouds wisp out in paintbrush strokes with all the numbers and Mrs. Belz, who talks in staccato. Each. Word. Separate. From. The. Last. She marks every word with sharp chalk smacks. I scroll through my Tree Book to an earlier page, when I didn't even know this school yet, and I see in the corner, all neat, because that's how you write when you start school: *Pin oak. Fruit. September.*

I turn away from the window and realize too late that Mrs. Belz's voice has stopped its steady pinprick. When I let my eyelashes flutter up, I see she's staring straight at me, waiting for the answer to a question I never heard.

"Can you repeat the question?" I ask, polite, the way Mom taught me.

"We're looking for *a*."

I see the long scribbled rows on the chalkboard, feeling eyes all around me. I'm the girl with no real place to live, too old to be wetting the bed, who doesn't know her algebra.

I catch Sabina Griffin's eye. She started in the middle of the year, while I started at the beginning. So she's the new girl, the girl nobody knows anything about, and for a second I think she's trying to show me what I can't find. Her hands are sprawled across the desk and a few fingers are curled under, but then she looks away, places her hands beneath her big puff skirt, and I think I must be imagining things. I look down at my notes and up again, hoping some answer will rise up in me.

All I can think is that *a* is already there. That *a* is *a* is *a* and nothing more.

"I don't know," I say, and it's like the whole room exhales. Meredith Crane's eraser starts flip-flopping again and Sabina Griffin waxes her huge rubber boots against the floor. Mrs. Belz shakes her head and reaches for the pages of her own notebook.

She makes a mark with a red-pen slap, and just as the bell rings, she snags me back. "Miss Quinn, let's talk."

Meredith snickers as she slides past.

"Things aren't picking up."

By *things* Mrs. Belz means *me*.

"I'm trying—"

Her hand goes up. "I'm putting in for a transfer for you to remedial math."

"Remedial?" Something in me falls.

"We're three-quarters of the way through the year. And you're—" She hesitates, softens. "Laps behind."

"Oh." I think of Adare, who gets yanked out of classes for special help. Is that what it's going to be like? "Can't I make it up, somehow? What if I pass the next test?"

She sighs, knowing we've been through this before.

"Not just pass. *Ace*," I say.

"You'd *have* to *ace* it in order to stay on track."

"One last chance," I beg.

"One last chance." Then she circles her desk, still looking for *a*.

Chapter 4

Ever since we moved to Ennis House, we have to meet Mom at the nearby park after school. Where Mom says it's safe. Because Ennis House isn't. Not with its broken locks and Old Lou on the steps and people grunting and yelling and shuffling in and out.

I have to walk a few minutes to pick up Adare, who waits at the steps of my old elementary school with her bright blue backpack at her feet. Kids spill out and some of the girls play Miss Mary Mack slap games while the others shout and wave. I wonder if there will be a day when Adare's got a friend, so I won't find her alone, like always.

She doesn't see me at first because her gaze runs up the streetlamp and stays there. I reach for her hand, and when it matches up with mine, she breathes in fast, like she just remembered she was alive.

"Hi." She grins wide. This is always her welcome, big

and bright and too in-your-face, even if she doesn't say much after that.

Then she holds my hand tight and I feel something sad in the pit of me. I shouldn't have lied.

"I'm sorry," I tell her. "It was me who wet the bed."

"Yeah."

But her grin stays the same. Warm and pretty and hers. In all the years I have held Adare close, I know nothing about how she really feels. I wish for one minute she'd snap out of who she is and become someone like the rest of us so I could know. As soon as I think the thought, I push it away. *Adare is who she is,* Mom always says. But I wonder every day who Adare really is.

Sometimes I go climbing around the neighborhood and drag Adare with me, but today we walk across the street and go straight to the park to wait for Mom. I drag Adare along the crisscross path and make my way back to my favorite spot. A pin oak. I'm waiting for spring to give it its leaves.

Adare sits at the roots and I take a look at the gray-brown bark. I make sure my backpack's tight on my shoulders, pull my sleeves down low, then hug the trunk with my elbows and thighs.

It was Daddy who taught me to climb, who told me the rules. His accent was full and wet, like Irish rain. Mom called it his *brogue.*

Always think in threes, he said, *and you'll never fall.*

Two feet, one hand. Two hands, one foot. He said that was all I needed to know.

Daddy knew about growing things. He worked in Brooklyn's gardens and came home dirt-stained and red-cheeked, slipping the radio to AM with its staticky old ballads. He'd reach for Mom's hand and spin her beneath his raised arm. He said Brooklyn dirt became his own sweet soil on the day he met her. While he studied plants and trees, she painted murals in community gardens—the art she did before Daddy died and she had to work long hours at the store. Because of her, he said, *Ireland might have been my home once, but America will be my home forever.*

Two feet, one hand. Two hands, one foot. I dizzy up the tree's straight spine, one nudge at a time, hands scratching, sneakers rubbing, until I reach the first branch. Then I pull up with two hands and tuck one foot inside the crook of each little V, branch to trunk. Up and up and up.

Daddy always said the best thing about a tree is getting *in* it. He said you might be able to stand over daisies, hold a rose in your hand, or look up at all the yellow suns in a sunflower field. But with a tree, you can sit in it and smell it and be in it. And maybe you can never put into words who or what it really is, but you can *know* it the way you can't know anything else.

That's why of all the growing things out there, I love trees best. They're someplace anyone can sit and stay, anytime they want.

I rest against the tree's back and let my thighs hug the thick branch. My sneakers sway above the earth. I scoot out to the edge and I don't even worry I'll fall. I don't feel stuck or caught. I just feel the way I did before Daddy died, before we kept picking up and going from one place to the next. I feel tucked-in safe.

We wait like this, longer than we ever have. Longer than we should. We wait until the sun falls down behind the harbor.

We wait for Mom to come in her khakis, her black hair in a loose ponytail, wearing her red shirt and name tag from the store. For her to call out, *Cora, Cora, come down.*

But she doesn't come.

One . . . two . . . three . . . I soar.

Chapter 5

When I reach the ground, it's cold. It's too late for us to be out. Too late for us to be alone. I know this. Adare's back is against the tree trunk and her legs are spread out wide. She's snaking her finger through the dirt and I huddle my arms around my chest.

"She's not coming," I say.

Adare is quiet, like always, smiling and swirling her finger like a magic wand.

"It's late and she's not coming," I say again. More to myself than to Adare.

Wherever we're living—doesn't matter whether it's Ennis House or Hoyt Street or on somebody's old couch—Mom tells us where to be. She sets her hands on my shoulders and makes me repeat street names. We wait where she tells us to wait, and she shows up. That's the way it's always been.

I start shivering and then my mind traces the streets toward Ennis House. I know Mom doesn't like us to be there without her, but it's the closest to a home we've got.

"We have to get back to Ennis House." I snatch Adare's hand from the dirt and she startles, with this shocked look on her face, like I stole her right out of her dreams. "We've gotta go," I say. "We can't be here."

She takes her hand back and shakes her head, her whispered voice a slow breeze. "Where's Mom?"

I spin my arms around. "Not here. See? Not here." And just saying it out loud makes the fact knock at my bones, and everything inside me pokes around in a jitter. Then I take her wrist in my fingers. Mom always says, with Adare we must be *gentle but stern.* "We have got to go," I say, firm.

She stands up straight and the dirt sticks to the sagging butt bottom of her polka-dot leggings. I watch the streetlamps glow orange inside the trees. The branches are battering up against the sky. It's colder now. It's dark. And I know the clock's edging to late. We haven't eaten since lunch.

When I wrap my hand around Adare's, she grabs on to my fingers the opposite way. It doesn't feel right. It feels like when you're forced into the buddy system on a field trip, how some hands don't fit together, how you have to fight to hold on the way you want or give in.

I give in, feeling caught up all wrong.

We walk the bumpy sidewalk. We pass the sticking-up fence of the church and the fancy ice cream shop with the logo that looks like a blueberry bush plunked on top of a cone. I don't look too close at anybody, just straight ahead, like I know I should, like nothing's the way it *isn't* supposed to be. The falafel shop has this smoky, charred, and golden smell and my stomach feels hollow and scared.

Mom's supposed to walk us and ask us about the day, how much homework I've got, what I drew on my hand, which I keep stuffed in my pocket, tucked safe. But if she's supposed to walk us, I'm supposed to stay put. Maybe it's me who messed up.

We reach the train underpass and the dark pulls over us, straight and tight, like a new sheet. I walk fast and squeeze Adare's hand, which clamps around mine. I don't want anyone to see us. I wish I could just close my eyes, disappear, open them, and end up where we're supposed to be.

A woman in plasticky pants swishes in front of us. An old man holds a bunch of paper bags as he swipes past. I study the ground, count sidewalks and streetlights and turns in my head. *Left, left, right.* The whoosh of the highway forces the wind across my cheeks.

A shadow jumps and I jump with it. Adare's hand fidgets out from mine. She takes off toward Miss Li's.

"Adare, you come back here!" I shout, but she's off, hair bouncing, moving like some little forest creature. Her high-tops tap-dance over the crunching grass along the old lot.

Chapter 6

"Adare!"

She sinks to the ground and I know what she's doing before I can stop it. One after the other the laced high-tops come off. You can't force a shoe on Adare. No way. Her bare feet have known every ground she's ever walked on, and at the end of the day, the dirt of all her everywheres becomes mud in the shower drain.

I run to the corner, thinking it's lucky we live where no one wants to or everyone would be looking at us and tsking, wagging their heads because it isn't normal, it isn't right. A little kid taking her shoes off in the middle of Brooklyn.

"Up!" I pull at her wrist, but she's giggling, and there go the socks, too, and I try to collect them when the shadow jumps again. She whizzes around, scrambles up, running barefoot, laughing hysterically, following whatever it is she sees, and I think, *Nuh-uh, no way am I chasing after this barefoot crazy kid. I'm done.*

It's dark and my pants are cold on the concrete. Her pink high-tops sit in my lap, with the sweaty socks rolled up into a ball.

I call out for her, but it's no use, she's running toward Miss Li's. Light shines from the tall glass windows of the shop. Stacks of detergent and toothpaste and lotto tickets. And I see, in the way the store lights up the street, that the shadow she's chasing is the smooth charcoal line of a cat.

She follows the cat while my fingers are wrapped in her laces. I stand up and wish Adare had been born different, but I push the wishing aside, like I always do, because we're here and it's late and Mom's missing—or we are—and I'm tired, so tired of trying to figure out where to be.

I slink on over, slow, to Miss Li's, and stand at the swinging door. Inside, Adare crouches at the beer refrigerators, where the cat is pawing at the silver and steel. It stretches its front legs out like it might leap away, but instead it starts licking its dark gray fur. Adare's cheek falls to her shoulder. She's mesmerized.

"No animals allowed!" Miss Li shouts, pointing to her handwritten signs behind the register—something about IDs and cigarettes, and no animals, and a big red Mrs. Belz X slashing through *American Express*.

"He's not ours," I say, but Miss Li's arm swings back

again and one skinny, wrinkled finger looks like it'll poke the sign straight into my eye.

"Out," she says, and her lips sag to her chin, like always, except for the one time Adare reached over the counter and touched the gold bracelet on her bone-thin wrist. Real gentle, with just one soft finger. Of course, Adare's smile, the way it has a habit of knowing people and calming them down, made Miss Li smile, too. *A gift from my son,* she said.

I look at her gold bracelet now. It's made to look like a ribbon, looped in a perfect bow. She wears it so tight, so close, her skin bunches up, tries to break free from behind it but never quite lets go.

I march over to Adare, who rests her head on her knees. She marvels at the cat like she's never seen one before, like we don't have a Sookie taking up room in our bed every night.

"Miss Li says no animals allowed." I look back to Miss Li for approval. She swings her arm around again to the sign.

"And we have to put your shoes on," I continue, reaching for her hand, but she snatches it away. So I try to take her foot and she giggles at the same time she whines like a baby, shifts her feet so they're tucked safe under her butt.

"Adare, please," I beg. "We gotta go."

She shakes her head, red hair sliding to her bare ankles,

like she'll slip to sleep right there, next to the stray cat, on the dirty floor of Miss Li's.

I pull at her wrist, but she screams out. I try to yank her up, but she laughs and wriggles her arm from my grasp. She slumps against the refrigerator and starts stroking the slippery gray fur. The cat's not skittish at all because Adare's *got a way*, like Mom says, with people and pets and all living things. But when I reach out, the cat jitters and tries to claw at me, teeth out, because whatever way Adare's got, I don't have.

I grab her wrist tight and pull, thinking I'll drag her straight across this store.

The cat's slithering along the bags of potato chips, then behind the register, where Miss Li reaches for a broom, hissing, "Scat!"

I hear a rubber screech across the floor and look up to see Sabina Griffin, who looks down at me like I'm a wad of gum stuck to her squeaking boots.

Chapter 7

'm confused at first, wondering what Sabina's doing at Miss Li's. I didn't think she lived over here. Actually, I don't know where she lives at all. Her hair's in two messy braids, like always. A dark brown eye, like rock, pokes from behind the strands, staring at me and my scene. I let go of Adare, who scrambles on her knees, looking for the cat. I know what Sabina's thinking, what everybody thinks about Adare: *What's wrong with her?*

And I turn my face off, the way you turn out the light. I take away every expression and make my face say, *Nothing. Nothing at all.*

Sabina swivels on her squealing boot. She pushes with her elbow against the tinkling door, and leaves.

The broom scratches the floor and Miss Li shrieks, "Out, out, out!"

The cat looks scared, its petal-green eyes drooping

low as it speeds toward the door, which looks like it'll shut right on the hook of its tail. Adare follows and I chase after her, shouting, "I'm sorry!" to Miss Li, whose red leopard glasses are bunched on her face. She's shaking her head, muttering in runaway words, "No animals allowed, says it right there, clear as day, I'm not running a zoo here, nuh-uh, look at the storefront, does it say *Miss Li's Menagerie*? I don't think so."

Then I'm out in the dark again. Sabina turns a corner. Gone in a flash.

The cat slips through a fence into an empty lot and Adare kneels down. Her fingers curl around the metal like she's caught behind bars.

"Look. It ran away," I scold. I know I should be soft, but everything in me has an edge. It's late, Mom's missing, and like it wasn't bad enough Sabina knowing I don't know where to find *a*, she had to see us acting like two lunatics in Miss Li's grocery.

Adare's face is still tearstained from when I stretched her legs and arms to try to get those shoes on. She runs her palm across her eyes and says in her sweet whisper, "But I love him."

"Not possible," I shoot back. "You don't even know him."

But when I look at her eyes, sad and wishing, searching for that cat, I think maybe it is possible to love someone or something you can't really ever get at. I think maybe it makes you love that someone or something even more.

I give in. Like always. "We'll find him," I say, even though I know we won't. He's a stray and all he knows is how to keep running away. "Someday. We will. Are you all right?"

Adare doesn't move, stares between the rings of the fence.

"We have to go . . ." I hesitate. *Home* isn't the right word. It never is. "Come on."

She nods. "Yeah." Then she shifts, sticks both her legs out in a V. I guess she's decided she's ready for her shoes.

Chapter 8

Ennis House is dark, and I hold Adare's hand tight, the way Mom would. The mush of cockroach is still there. That's four days.

Old Lou doesn't make way for us, not this time, not without Mom. He sits on the last step and his bottom takes up the whole width of the stairs. I don't know why he sits here like this. One long wait for nobody.

Behind him, echoes slide down the banister. His eyes are two small squints. A crooked scar from the corner of one eye slashes past his cheek to his ear. I'd be scared if I hadn't already decided I couldn't be.

I think he smiles, but I'm not sure. His voice is ragged and old and it moves slow, like guiding a cane forward. "Where's your mama?"

I try to pretend like I know, like she's where I wish her to be. "Here."

"Really? That so?"

I nod, but of course he would know better. He knows the coming and going of everyone, and if he hasn't seen her, then she's not upstairs, and if she's not upstairs, I won't know what to do.

"Where you coming from?" he asks.

"School," I say.

"Bit late. For school." And this time, he smiles. I'm sure of it.

So I breathe in deep and ask, "Can I get by?"

He holds his hand out, dirt trapped under his nails. "Gotta pay the toll."

Toll? All I have is my school ID and my lunch card. That's it, and I don't think that's what he's looking for.

Words are stuck in me. I wish I never left that tree.

I shake my head. I don't understand the game he's playing.

I feel Adare clench beside me, see her chest rise up. She's holding her breath again and I close my eyes as if that will set it free.

I want to get upstairs—*have* to get upstairs—because we don't have any other place to go.

My backpack slips from my shoulder, like a nudge, so I let it fall to my wrist, twist the straps, unzip it, like I'm looking for cash I don't have. Just notebooks and one giant textbook for third-period science. We're on unit 3: "Kingdoms of Life." The first question is, *What makes something alive?*

With Adare's breath caught, I can't seem to find my own. The two of us are bunches of tiny cells stacked up and tucked under, and if we don't let the world in and out, if we hold the air in our cheeks, if we never let go, we're a part of nothing. We disappear.

So I feel around, not knowing what I need, only that I need something to get past him. In the back flap of my pack, my Tree Book is smooth and soft.

I root around until I feel something at the tips of my fingers. An acorn I collected last fall.

It's smooth and cold and wears its little cap. Before I know what I'm doing, I'm handing it over, offering it up. Because what else is there?

When I place it in his palm, he clutches my hand, quick. When I let go of the acorn, he lets go of me, and I take my hand back. Adare's breath is still jammed.

He looks at it in his swollen, wrinkled palm. His lips flatten and I'm sure it isn't what he's looking for.

But he laughs and his laugh is crumpled up with a cough, like he had to force it out.

I feel Adare's breath release.

He stands up. He balls the acorn up in his fist, gives a laugh that's more like a *Hooey,* and slaps a thigh with the other palm.

Then he extends his arm like it's a bow, like we're two queens. "Go on."

I don't think Adare and I have ever run so fast and sure

up the stairs, past Mrs. Johnson's yelling and the whiff of Fred C.'s brown-bag fast food. We run so fast, I hardly remember what we're running toward until we reach five, my calves stinging, my lungs aching, and it feels like the two of us crash into the big red door.

The lock's broken and the door is off the hinges. When I look inside, most of our stuff is in a heap. My greenhouse sits in shards of glass, all the little true leaves lost in a mound of damp brown dirt. The rest of what we have is spread out like a fallen clothesline. The breeze from the open window sends it all flying around.

Adare runs to the window. Her tea box is smashed on the sill. She shakes it. It's empty. All of her gifts are gone.

She dips to the floor, where her peanut stash sits crushed. She scoops up the dust of peanuts and looks up at me.

I don't know what to say.

I hear Sookie mewing, scared, underneath the dresser.

Chapter 9

Adare and I sit shoulder to shoulder on the lumpy mattress. Her polka-dot leggings shoot straight out while my striped leggings bunch up to my chest. I balance my Tree Book on my wobbly knees.

I close my eyes and dream about the tree of heaven. Giant naked arms reaching to the sky, waiting for a hug that never comes. My pencil stretches the branches to the ends of each page. It slips off the edge of the notebook.

I can't think of a *next*. I can only push the arms of my tree farther and farther, until we're shielded in a web of twisted vines, one giant hug to keep us safe.

When I open my eyes, my pencil hovers in the air. I point the tip back to the lined notebook, and as I press down, the point snaps.

Everything stays unfinished.

I rest my head against the wall. I keep getting a whiff of

the cat pee, the sounds of feet rambling on the stairs, and the mash of all kinds of yucky smells. Shouts and conversation spill out in gushing half-words.

"What're we gonna do?" I say out loud. "Everything's a mess."

"Yeah." Adare rubs her eyes, then sinks lower to the mattress, nuzzles her head at my shoulder. Sookie scrapes at the floorboards.

Then I hear more stomping, feet getting louder at each flight, and someone's at five, and I follow white rubber shoes, closer and closer, khaki pants, a gray puff coat, Mom's swinging ponytail.

Her arms are around us before I can stand. Her bag slips past her arm to the mattress with a thud. She's shaking. I'm so relieved that tears well up in me. My Tree Book is a smash at my chest. It's like my pencil branches found their way around us.

"You're here," she says at the same time I say, "Where were you?"

She holds us tight, fitting her head between ours. She speaks like a slow leak. "You meet me at the park," she says, her warm breath at my neck. "Always."

"I'm sorry," I whisper. "I thought—" But I don't know what I thought. That she had forgotten us. Me.

"The store— I had no choice. I tried to leave on time." She shakes her head. "It doesn't matter. You're okay. That's what matters." She pulls back, holds Adare's chin in her hand. Adare's smile is so wide, you could fall in. "You're okay, right?"

"Yeah."

Then Mom looks around, at the mess, at the swinging door and the broken lock, and asks what we've been wondering. "Sweet Jesus, what happened?"

"It was like this," I say, and for a moment I think I have to convince her. "It wasn't us."

She tries to close the broken door. She twists the doorknob and it spins like a loose wheel.

She's gentle but stern. "See, Cora, this is why you can never come here alone."

I watch her gaze circle the room. Mom's face, you can't read it. Her expressions have a way of going missing.

But I know what will happen. I know, as she sets her teakettle on the hot plate, that the three of us are as good as gone.

Chapter 10

"Willa's?" I ask, confused.

Mom's nod is quick, like she's not even sure herself. She's got her hand wrapped around Adare's wrist. Clumsily packed bags dip from her elbows and bulge over her shoulders like a humpback. I clutch my backpack and a laundry bag full of clothes while we stand on the corner of Smith and Ninth Streets to hail a cab, something we never do, but Mom says these are *special circumstances*.

I remember Willa visiting us at our old place on Hoyt Street. She was giraffe-tall and I remember the weird way her knees bunched up when she sat on Mom's beanbag chair. She eyed us and our place like she was Dorothy landing in Oz, except we were in black and white and she was in color. When Mom and Willa talked, Mom's Texas accent crept in, like some tired, moping dog.

"Can't we stay at Jessie's?" I ask. She's one of Mom's

old artist friends and I like her purple couch. I like the way we sit out on her fire escape at night while she blows smoke rings into the sky with her cigarettes.

Mom shakes her head. "Jessie's gone." She says it like a magician's *Poof!* The way a lot of Mom's artist friends disappear.

"But we barely know Willa," I argue.

"She's my oldest friend, Cora." She raises her arm in the chill of the air. "Some people are like family."

Family. Something I've been told repeatedly we don't have.

But before I know it, I'm rubbing against the musty leather of the cigarette-smelling cab, slicing through the streets to some shiny new condo towers in Downtown Brooklyn, and standing in a chandeliered lobby, where a man in a suit stands behind a desk and asks us who we're here to see.

"Willa Rose," Mom says.

He picks up a telephone and dials, pokes his chin out at us. "And who should I say is here to see her?"

Mom hesitates before she says, "Liana."

He repeats it into the phone. "Ms. Rose, Liana is here to see you."

Mom looks like she's holding her breath and I look from her to the man, to the way his mustache twitches, to the mirrored walls, reflecting the light and us, with all our things in a lump at our feet.

He pokes his chin at us again. "Go on up."

I watch Mom's shoulders fall, like she's relieved, and we lug our things up a fancy elevator. Velvety carpet lines its way down a narrow sliver of a hallway where Willa stands in an open door.

Her arms are folded and she looks past us into Mom's eyes, which don't look straight at anybody for too long, and Mom says, "You said if we ever needed a place to stay . . ."

Willa nods and her lips curve up into a cautious smile. "You're both so big. It was only last year I saw you, wasn't it? And look at you."

"They grow like weeds," Mom says.

Adare chimes in loud with a big grin. "Hi."

Willa looks taken aback, but she smiles and it's like how people always come around to Adare. "Hello."

We stand this way at the door, like going isn't an option—like staying might not be one, either. I don't know how I feel about Willa, not yet. She doesn't wrap us up into suffocating hugs like Jessie does, leading us into her smoky, cluttered apartment, half studio, half living space, with stained coffee cups stacked in the sink. Willa just kind of flings her arm into her apartment and says, "Come on in."

I watch Mom and Willa exchange glances, like they're trying to talk to each other without making a sound. Then I walk in and take a look at the apartment.

Willa's place is shiny new and it's all modern, with

clean windows in the shape of a geometry lesson. Not like the ripped-up chaos of Ennis House or the cooped-up apartment we lived in on Hoyt Street.

No, Willa's home is all crisp and clean. Everything's made of smooth light-colored wood. She doesn't keep a lot of things. A white apron on a hook and a painting on the wall that's mint green with brown scratchy paint shadows of leaves and a canoe.

We're surrounded by rectangles of glass. They reflect the city like mirrors and make everything look the way it does when you snap a photo too fast in the dark.

I look up at Willa. She wears clothes that seem expensive. She's Mexican American, like Mom, and her hair is dark and shining.

My own hair hangs from my head like the shreds of a bristly rope. I feel like a ghost next to someone so pretty.

"Did something happen?" Willa asks.

"Someone broke in—" I start, but Mom interrupts.

"I'll explain later," she says. "It wasn't safe."

Willa nods, like she understands. "You take my room. I'll stay out here." She points to the couch. It's pure white and there aren't even any pillows.

Mom shakes her head. "No, of course not. We'll stay out here."

"You sure?"

"Of course. It's fine. Right, girls?"

I shrug while Adare says, "Yeah."

"We're already inconveniencing you enough," Mom continues.

"Don't be silly." Willa opens a closet and I've never seen so many white blankets and sheets, stacked up all tidy. She starts stuffing pillowcases, unfolding blankets, and spreading them out.

Mom holds out our soft patchy quilt.

I take it from her and crumple it in my arms, then sit on the couch and curl up in it, my head on the couch's arm. "We got what we need."

Willa looks at the quilt's worn edges, loose threads in rows of silk fringe. She smiles. I wonder if she has to fake it. "Well, if you need anything else . . ." She sets the linens in a neat pile.

Then we look at one another.

Adare holds Sookie in her arms. I can hardly believe the fussy-faced cat let Adare swoop her up from the floor and carry her down the stairs and out the door of Ennis House to here.

"Is she friendly?" Willa asks.

Adare grins up at her. "Yeah."

Friendly is not what I would call Sookie. But I let Willa believe it. I don't want her smile to disappear.

Mom stands in a heap of all of our belongings, which are stuffed into a few duffel bags and backpacks. "Let's talk," she tells Willa, and I wonder what she'll say about all that happened to us tonight.

I sit rumpled in our quilt.

"Settle in first. You can stay in my room," she tells Mom. "Like when we were girls. A sleepover." Her laugh is clear and round, not the smallest husk in her voice.

Mom's smile is brief. She nods. But her dark eyes hold on to the heaviness of the day. "I'll be in in a minute."

"There're some leftovers in the fridge, if you'd like." Willa's brown eyes sparkle silver when she speaks. She doesn't just say *Good night,* she says, "Good night, ladies," and it makes me feel as if we're wrapped in the proper language of a beautiful old book.

Willa walks the narrow hallway to her bedroom. The hardwood floors are smooth. She's so tall, and the length of her, the way her arms dangle to her knees, makes it feel like she's taking over the whole room even when she's walking away.

Mom sits beside me and nuzzles into the space between cushions. She seems smaller than when we left Ennis House, her coat even bulkier on her tiny frame. Her hair is straight, spooling silk. She motions for Adare to sit on the other side of her. Adare does not let go of Sookie for a moment.

"I'm sorry I was late," Mom tells us.

"I'm sorry we left the park," I say. "We should have waited."

Mom doesn't know about Miss Li and the charcoal cat. She doesn't know about Old Lou and the acorn. It seems like, all of a sudden, she doesn't know much of anything at all.

I can tell she doesn't have a *next*. I can tell by the way she settles into the crack of the couch cushion. The way she reached for that dangling lock, the pieces of my greenhouse, and her fallen teakettle. It isn't the first time we've had to live on someone else's couch. I keep wondering when it will be our last.

Sometimes I think Mom doesn't know how to stay.

"How come we've never been here before?" I ask, looking around the room. The Brooklyn Bridge is a slope of glowing light reflected against the tall glass.

"We're not looking for a handout, Cora."

I nod. I know this. Some of the kids get free school lunch, but Mom says that's *not for us*.

I wonder, *Then who's it for?*

"It's all going to turn out just fine," Mom reassures me. "Don't worry."

I try not to. I always do. But it gnaws at me, gets at my mind—this idea we don't belong anywhere. "But where's the right place for us?" I ask.

She sighs. "Since Daddy died, Cora, no place feels right. But I keep trying. That's all I can do."

Adare strokes Sookie's fur and tries to cuddle against the stiff cushions. Mom takes my palm, holding it in her smooth hands. She leans into my ear and I feel the warmth of her voice. "What do we have today?"

I had almost forgotten the small scribble in my palm. Normally, I would tell her about Mrs. Belz and all the answers I don't have, the lost letters I can't find. But my story seems small. "It's the letter *a*," I tell her.

She smiles. "A beginning."

But it doesn't feel like one at all.

Chapter 11

Morning comes early and fast and I wake with my Tree Book clutched to my stomach. I sit up and adjust my eyes.

Mom brushes her hands across our shoulders and makes us tiptoe over as the sun rises through the wraparound windows.

It stretches pink across the sky.

Adare smashes her nose against the cold glass and I moan, "It's too *eaaarly*," but Mom shushes me.

We wear our clothes from the day before, the butt of Adare's polka-dot pants sagging and one leg of my striped leggings all bunched up at my knee, but I'm too lazy to fix it. Mom wears her shirt from the store. She lets it fall to her bare thighs.

"Is Willa mad we're here?" I ask.

Mom shakes her head. "Willa is like a sister."

If she's like a sister, I wonder why we only see her once a year.

"I *thought* I heard someone." Willa swoops in. Her pajamas are a matching set of purple silk pants and a flowy button-down. "I should remember—Liana loves her mornings," she says.

"Your mother loves her mornings," she repeats, like we don't know. She makes her way to the kitchen. "Coffee?"

Mom shakes her head. "Do you have tea?"

"Tea?" Her laugh is all tittery. "Since when do you drink tea?"

"Since always."

"What would Meema say? She loved her coffee. With cinnamon."

Willa turns to Adare and me. "Your *abuela*'s house—it smelled like heaven.

"Remember her *marranitos*?" she asks Mom.

"Cookies with molasses," she tells us. "They're shaped like little pigs."

I look at Mom. Her face does not move away from the window as the sky fades from pink to a line of white.

"We didn't know Meema," I say softly.

"I know," Willa says, eyeing Mom through her strands of thick hair. Then she laughs. "She would marvel at two little Brooklyn girls. *City slickers.*"

I wonder what she means, but before I can ask, Mom says, "Meema loved the easy flow of country life."

"But no life is easy," Willa says, and I watch her eye all of our belongings sitting in a heap. She takes a look at my one-leg-up leggings and I quickly straighten them to my ankles.

"She would be happy I came here and married someone I loved," Mom says. "That I painted. That I tried."

Willa wipes her coffee cup clean with a towel. Her hands on her hips, she says, "Well . . . we should discuss logistics."

"The attorney and her logistics." Mom shakes her head, but I see an amused smile at her lips.

"How will they get to school from here?"

"They'll walk."

"Don't be silly. They'll ride the subway. It's only two stops."

"For real?" I ask. Then I look between them both. "We're too tall to ride free," I tell Willa.

"I don't know," Mom starts. "Is it safe?"

"Of course it's safe," Willa replies. "We'll get them MetroCards."

I notice how she says *we'll,* but I know she means *I'll.*

Mom's weird about MetroCards. We're supposed to get them from school, but we didn't have proof of address at sign-up. "Absolutely not," she says, and I see that the discussion is over. "They'll walk. The subway takes just as long, when you account for all the waiting."

Willa puts her hands up in the air. "Fine."

Then she asks, "What time do you get home from the store?"

"It's different every day, but for the most part I take the early shift. I meet the girls around four-thirty."

Willa rummages through drawers. "I have spares."

She hands a key to Mom and the other she holds out to me. It lights the mirrors in Adare's eyes, and before I can take it, Adare snatches the jagged end and clutches it with two hands. She smiles up at us.

"She likes the silver," I explain.

Willa smiles. "Me too."

"We'll be out of your hair soon," Mom interjects. "It won't be long."

Willa tosses the towel over her shoulder. "It'll be what it is." Then she turns to me. "Tea?" she asks.

I look at Mom's purple cup steaming, then at Willa's empty mug. "Coffee," I say as Mom interjects, "Since when—" and I add, "With cinnamon."

"Don't worry," Willa tells Mom. "A little can't hurt."

When I follow Willa into the kitchen, she opens the cupboard and takes out a mug with bold black lettering: *Brooklyn Law.* Then she reaches in a drawer and rummages around. She sets out two spoons and clutches my hand tight in hers.

I feel the crisp, folded bills and hear her whisper, "For a MetroCard."

When I look at the money, when I wonder, when I say,

"Oh no, we can't," Willa puts her finger to her lips and smiles.

I know I shouldn't take it. I should place it on the table and walk the twenty minutes to school the way Mom wants. But we're always sleeping on couches when we should be sleeping in beds. We're always walking, dragging ourselves from one spot to the next, when we should be riding the subway.

I don't smile, even if I wanted to. That would make it too much like *our little secret,* which is what it seems Willa wants. But I don't let go. I can't. I place the money in the pocket of yesterday's hoodie.

Chapter 12

For the first time, I can't wait to leave school so I can get back to where we're staying. Willa mentioned something about ordering Thai food or sushi from a stack of takeout menus. Her soap smells like coconuts and there's a whole new set of trees I can survey from up high.

So I rummage through my locker, looking fast over my rainbow—the color codes for each subject. It's the way the teachers taught us to organize our books. English is purple. Science is green. Math is sky blue, but I feel it should be black.

The smooth yellow MetroCard sits at the foot of my locker, in a clear pocket case that came with my backpack. I put it there after the machine sucked up Willa's money and spit it out at me. It feels like a bad secret. I stuff it in my pack.

I clutch my Tree Book to my chest and slam my locker quick. There's the shriek of rubber against the waxy floors and someone knocks at my shoulder.

"Hey!" I say.

It's Sabina Griffin, skidding the hallways, like she's on a skateboard. Her chin is tucked in her coat and her braids fall from a droopy wool hat that slips to her lashes. Our eyes catch and I expect her to look away, but she doesn't. She stares me down like the two of us know something and share it.

I realize, for the first time, she doesn't wear a book bag. Never does. Her books are trapped under her arm, papers poking from folders.

She brushes past me and I watch her make her way out the door. I want to find out what she was doing at Miss Li's, so I take off after her. Outside, the world brightens from the dark hallways. I watch her as she hops the steps and beelines for the metal fence, where she swoops down, smoothing a crumpled paper in her hands.

"Whatcha got there?" I call out, between kids scuffling on the pavement and parents talking to each other at pickup, something Mom's not usually here to do.

I make my way closer and she tucks the paper in her skirt pocket. Then she grabs my hand, all urgent-like. "Spot me."

"Spot you?"

Before I can say anything, her arms are down and her legs are up. Her huge boots slap the fence behind her and I find myself catching her legs. "What're you doing?"

"It's an *inversion*."

"A what?"

"A handstand."

"Is it, um, necessary?" I hold her ankle with one hand.

"I need a new view," she tells me, then flips backward to her feet and stands up. All the blood has rushed to her face. She clutches my hand. "I'm in, like, this total rut."

"A rut?"

"School. It's the *same* thing. Every. Single. Day."

"Yeah, well, that's kinda how it goes."

"Doesn't that bum you out?"

I shrug. "Not really. It's . . . I don't know. *School*. What are you expecting?"

She sighs dramatically. "A miracle."

"Whatcha got?" I ask again, pointing to her pocket.

She takes out the paper and holds it in her steady palm. "Notes. Words. Things like that. I'm collecting them." She crumples the paper and stuffs it in her pocket. Before I can ask more, she gestures to my Tree Book. "What's that?"

I try to think how to explain. No one's ever asked. "A field journal," I say. "My dad's, before he died. Now mine. I draw tree maps," I say, like it's a thing.

She doesn't even question it, just smiles. "Cool."

"I saw you," I tell her. "At Miss Li's. You live over there?"

She nods. "On the canal. Where do you live?"

I wonder how to answer. Yesterday I could have said I live at Ennis House, with the smack of cockroach and a smashed-up greenhouse. Today I can say I live in a giant Rapunzel tower in Downtown Brooklyn, next to the cupcake shop Willa told us about. She says they have cupcakes with *the best* names. "Nowhere special," I say, and leave it at that.

"Why do you keep track of trees?" she asks.

"Why do you collect notes?" I ask quick, and smile.

Her stare is wide-eyed, huge. "Just do." Then she's off again, walking the perimeter of the fence, fast, like she's following a trail. "I'll see you Monday," she says, like we talk all the time, like we're best friends forever, like obviously we hang out every day. "Right?"

I remember Sabina in math class when I was looking for *a,* how it seemed like she was helping me. I like her handstands and her collecting things, so I say it back. "Right."

She breaks into a huge grin and I watch her fingers skim the pavement, searching, I guess, for whatever it is she's looking for.

Chapter 13

Adare and I ride the subway that afternoon and it feels like we're flying free. Mom's right that it takes just as long as walking, but I'm glad I took Willa's money. I get to slip the card fast at the turnstile and the two of us flip through like tumbling acrobats. I get to hold Adare's hand and race down the stairs, matching my legs up with hers. We check to see who ran their markers over the subway posters and drew bunny ears or buckteeth on the actors. Then we air-trace our fingers over the map, counting stops, like Mom taught us years ago, *just to double-check.*

When we get into the subway car, it's crowded and we're caught in the stink of somebody's armpit. Music's leaking from somebody's earbuds.

When the train leaves, I hold on to the slick, greasy pole and spin around and around. As the train moves forward, my feet try to stay in place and it feels like I'm on a whirling carousel.

Then we push out, spin the turnstile, and race up the stairs. When we reach the top step, the air is crisp, and the outside comes at us, sky and pavement, top to bottom, like a zooming camera. We slam our feet in unison as if we crossed a finish line.

"You know the way?" I ask.

Adare nods, real fast. "Yeah."

I notice trees as we go, marking them off in my head so I can write them down later, but there are no trees in the front of Willa's building. Only the mustached doorman and an elevator that dings at every floor. We soar, almost to the top, and then we're let out to the hallway. There's no Old Lou, no sweet whiff of burger or the Johnsons stamping their voices into the walls. All the doors are closed and they each have one gold letter that drums the alphabet until we get to G.

I picture Willa's apartment and the way we've invaded it. The old quilt tossed on the couch . . . our bags slumped in a corner like sacks of old potatoes . . . our school-books . . . Adare's filthy butterfly wings strapped across an arm of the couch.

I let Adare turn the key and then peer into the living room. Everything but Sookie has been hidden away and Willa's apartment looks like it did when we first arrived. I swallow hard. So Willa's already annoyed by our stuff. She probably can't wait to get us out.

Our backpacks slip to the floor and we head straight for the glass windows. From this high we can see Brooklyn spread out in gray-brown rows. The East River slides beneath the bridge. Manhattan sits across it, all Lego-stacked and dotted with shadowed squares of windows. Adare runs her fingers across the glass like she's touching it all.

I point at the outside window ledge. "See anything?" I ask.

She shakes her head. She knows what I mean. Her crows will be looking for a new place to leave their gifts.

It's impossible for me to count trees from here. There are too many. They swirl the edge of the park in big brown batches. Their branches reach out to the gold lines of the bridge like a rope.

"I want to stay here forever," I tell Adare. "Don't you?"

"Okay. Yeah."

Sookie rests at her feet with her fur against the warm glass. Her eyes are two sleepy blue slits as she curls up in the space between Adare's shoes.

"I think even Sookie likes it here," I say because for some dumb reason I feel the need to convince Adare that this is where we belong. "She likes it anywhere *you* are."

Adare's smile is wide and toothy. She giggles, like I've uncovered a great secret.

I think of Adare's peanuts. "Your crows. Are they going to come back?"

"Yeah," she says. I wonder if she's really sure or if she's just *yeah*ing me to death.

We watch the view change. The sun drips yellow at the tips of each silver building. The tugboats cross and disappear to where we can't see. The Staten Island ferry glows orange, then becomes a speck and fades.

After we get tired of gazing out, we go to the refrigerator. Willa said we can have anything we like. Mom told us, *Don't be vultures.* So we settle somewhere in between. One snack each. Adare wants celery with peanut butter. But Willa's got the natural kind, all dry and clumpy, so I choose cinnamon applesauce.

It's cold and sweet and I jam the spoon at the smallest stuck bits. When it's finished, I scrape the little plastic container to get all I can. I have to have everything. Adare leaves peanut butter on her plate and puts the plate in the sink, like we were told, but I can't stand the thought of it sitting there and nobody eating it. Dry as it is, I run my fingers along the smooth white plate and find every inch of peanut butter. It sits all wadded and gummy in the pit of my stomach. But I get it all.

Next we do our homework on the couch. Which, for me, means worksheets. One after the other. Questions filled out in my crooked, scratchy handwriting. I stare at all the numbers like one day they're going to make sense.

For Adare, it means sitting with her to-do list that gets sent home in her backpack. I say *sitting with* because that's what she does until I snatch the sheet and look it over. "Adare, which you gonna start with?"

Her shoulders rise up and fall and her eyes have this wide way of looking at me like she's trying to figure me out.

"I've got to study, Adare." I poke my finger at the list. "Pick one."

Adare can read, but she doesn't read right. She gets pulled from one specialist to another because, when it comes to Adare, nobody can get enough of the word *special*. I hate the word because, when it comes to Adare, what they really mean is *different*. What they really mean is *wrong*.

"How about this one?" I suggest.

"Okay, yeah," she says before I even read it out.

"You have to read the story and write what you have in common with the main character."

She smiles at me and her hair falls to her soft cheeks.

"Do you understand? Read the story. Then write what you have in common with the main character. We'll write it together, okay?" I think how she writes like a first grader, in big block letters, the spelling all wrong.

She doesn't look away, but she doesn't answer.

"You have to do the assignments, Adare."

"Yeah."

She leans back, arms above her head, letting them rest

on the couch's white canvas. The falling sunlight dances across her face.

"You have to fill out the answers. That's how it works." I dangle the to-do list before her eyes. She doesn't even blink.

I used to think this made Adare dumb, the way she stared back blank, like she didn't understand. But sometimes I think Adare is smarter than any of us. Sometimes I think she has it all figured out.

Because I can't sit with cats and rip my shoes off when I don't feel like wearing them. I can't hand back worksheets empty. I can't even fail a test without Mrs. Belz transferring me to remedial math.

"Adare," I say. "Do you know how lucky you are to be you?"

She looks at me long and hard and for a minute I think she'll tell me I'm wrong, because I can never figure out whether being Adare is good or bad or if I'll ever find an answer to that kind of question at all.

Instead, she laughs, from deep inside her belly, her shoulders shaking like a soft wind.

Chapter 14

That night, Mom promises us a *fancy* dinner from Willa's kitchen, so I wear all my favorite things at once—yellow leggings, green shorts, and a purple tee with lavender hearts.

Mom wears the crisp white apron from the hook and hands me a wooden spoon. "You'll be my sous-chef," she says.

Then she curls her black hair around her finger and tacks it in place behind her head with a bobby pin. One small strand slips away.

Willa watches from up against the wall, in flowy black pants and earrings that fall to her neck.

"You look very elegant," I tell her.

"This is *Corporate Willa*," she jokes.

"There are other Willas," Mom tells us. "Like *Pro Bono Willa*."

"On the weekends, I work on cases for free," Willa explains.

"She loves a charity case." There's something sour in Mom's voice, like gnawing on a lemon, and I know she's talking about us.

Adare sinks to the kitchen floor, stroking Sookie. Her legs are out in a big wide V and her smelly bare feet stick up in the air. I wonder why she can't keep her socks on.

"*Frijoles charros,* huh?" Willa asks with a small smile.

Mom nods. "Mexican cowboy beans."

"Like your meema used to make."

"The very same."

I have a memory, in some old cloud, of Mom making things on the stove, but I was too little to remember it right.

"You've had this before?" I ask Willa.

She smiles. "Of course. I was at your mother's house for dinner all the time."

I try to picture Mom and Willa as little girls. The same dark hair, sliding to their elbows. Willa so tall and Mom short beside her. The two of them, playing slap games at recess, words and hands waiting to meet.

"What can I do?" Willa asks.

But Mom flicks her hand at the air, like she's brushing away crumbs. "Nothing, nothing. You relax."

She moves around the kitchen like a dancer. One leg balanced on tiptoe on the smooth tile, the other tipping back as she reaches into a cabinet. She swirls from the counter to the stovetop, onions raining from her fingers into a pan. We haven't had a real kitchen for the longest time, and I wonder, *If we did, would she flit about like this every night?*

"What do I do?" I ask.

She leads me to a tall pot, places her hand around my fingers, which I curl up around the spoon. "You. Stir."

I peer into the pot, hot steam disappearing at my cheeks, watching the beans rise and fall. Sometimes we have pasta and jar sauce. Frozen meals defrosted in a microwave. Never Mexican cowboy beans from a meema we've never known.

"How was school this week?" Mom asks me.

"Fine," I say. But I don't mention my maybe new friend, Sabina Griffin. I just stir it up inside me the way I spin the beans. Sabina Griffin and her blur, running along the fence the way a skater would, her head down and braids over her eyes. It's better if she stays invisible. A perfect secret kept safe. So when we leave her behind, like we leave everything behind, it'll be like she was never there.

"Remember Allister Ruffin?" Willa asks. "I was thinking of him the other day. I don't know why."

Mom nearly snorts, one hand on her hip as she uses tongs to flip meat with the other. "The thief."

"Thief?" I ask. "What'd he steal?"

Willa takes her finger and curls it through Adare's auburn hair. "A bird's nest."

"Um, okay."

"It's true," Mom says. "He was a climber. Like you."

Something in me feels proud when she says it. *A climber.*

"But nests aren't easy to spot in South Texas," Willa continues. "We didn't have winters like here. The trees don't always lose their leaves."

"So how'd you know he took one?" I ask.

"He wasn't very discreet about it. He used it for an awful prank."

"He placed it in a tree," Mom says. "Put eggs in it. Eggs—like from the supermarket. And he pretended the nest was tangled up with a kite. Then he got somebody to help him untangle his kite and the eggs fell on my head."

I laugh. "That's pretty funny."

Mom shakes her head. "Not when you're trying to get the yolk out of your hair before school."

Willa's laugh starts out small, but soon she brings her fingers to her mouth, trying to stop it from fluttering too far. Mom turns to the meat, its juice sputtering over the high heat, but with her hair back, I see the bloom of her smile.

I like Mom and Willa as almost-sisters. I like that they share the same story, one looping ribbon that used to be theirs.

The sauce bubbles. A thick, popping, breathing, living pot of spices and beans. The smoky smell catches the kitchen air.

When we sit down at the wood table, Willa wishes for tortillas. "We had them with every meal."

"Or a stack of white bread, if we ran out," Mom says, and they both laugh.

"It smells the way I remember it," Willa says, and I imagine Meema's cinnamon-smelling home, the way Willa talked about it like it was her own.

Mom sits across from me. Her eyes are bright and she looks happier than I've ever known her to look. Like, maybe, we've finally found somewhere to belong.

I place my hands around the bowl. *Frijoles charros.* All of a sudden, we're living as if we have a past.

"How come we never came here before?" I ask later that night. Adare and I are sitting on the couch, fitting across it just right. Mom sits on the floor while I braid her hair.

"I love Willa," she tells me. "Like a sister. But we're different."

"Like how Willa works in some fancy building and you work at the store?" I ask.

"Yeah. Like that." She curls her knees up and rests them on the rug. "She doesn't always like the choices I make."

"Choices?" I ask.

"So many we have to make in life. Like school and jobs

and picking the people you want to love." Her voice falls away. "I know it's not so easy to understand. But you have to make your own choices."

I nod, thinking how I choose to keep some things secret, how I don't always know what I should and shouldn't say.

"Sometimes you make bad choices. But they're still yours. And it's better than people thinking they know what's best for you, when they might not."

"Like Tilda?" I ask. Mom's meetings with Tilda always end with Mom telling her she's wrong.

"I've met with Tilda. She's working on getting a new placement for us."

I set one piece of hair at her neck, not wanting to hear about any *placement*, just wanting to stay right here at Willa's. I loop the soft black strand between my fingers.

It was Daddy who braided my hair before school. He'd take my messy mop and smooth each part with his big, clumsy thumbs. He'd fumble through the knots and tell me about Irish brides braiding their hair for *power and luck*, which I didn't need because I had both already. Even when Mom offered him her hair ties from the drugstore, he'd use crumbly old rubber bands from the garden.

On Palm Sunday, he'd do the same with his palm leaves, turning them around each other into neat, pretty twists. Adare and I would sit between him and Mom in the church's stuffy wooden pew and I'd try to do the same with my leaves. They'd end up all crooked and lumpy. But Daddy's looked like a ribbon of beautiful silk.

"Did you wear a braid in your hair when you married Daddy?" I ask.

"What made you think of that?"

"Daddy said Irish brides wear braids. For power and luck."

"I wore my hair wild." She turns back. "Like yours." She says it with a smile.

"Was Willa there?" I wonder. "When you got married?"

She shakes her head.

"Was Meema?" I ask.

"No."

"How come?"

"Meema had already died."

"And Willa?"

"She didn't approve of your father."

"Why not?"

"Oh, I don't know. He talked too much, he didn't make a lot of money, he was dirty all the time."

We both laugh and I imagine Daddy in his muddy work boots, his fingernails caked with dirt, no matter how hard he scrubbed them in the bathroom sink.

"She wanted me to marry some rich somebody. In a suit."

I laugh again, but I see Mom's not laughing.

"Did you get in a fight?" I wonder.

She shakes her head. "It wasn't like that. We just saw each other less. We weren't the same kids we were in Texas anymore."

"You never talk about Texas," I tell her.

She flits her hand. "It was a lifetime ago."

"But we didn't know about *frijoles charros*. We didn't know about the cinnamon. We don't even know what Texas looks like. Right, Adare?"

Adare turns away from the window and looks at me. She surprises me when she nods and says all quiet, "Yeah."

"See?"

"Well, there's a river in San Antonio," Mom begins. She sticks her hand out straight, then swerves it back and forth, like the head of a nosy fish. "It runs right through the city. And at night the lights have a certain way of hitting the water while they poke through the trees."

"What kind of trees?"

She swirls her hand. "Oh, all kinds. Cypress and sycamore. Persimmon. Pecan."

I take stock of Mom's trees and tick them off in my mind. Not like we have here.

"And live oaks," she adds. "They're supposed to be the best climbing trees."

"How come?"

She extends her arm out, as if she might take a bow.

"The branches are long. I bet you could walk them like a tightrope."

I hear Willa emerge from her room in her silk pajamas. I look to Mom, who smiles and doesn't seem worried that Willa might have heard what she said about her. Willa peeks her head around the corner, not looking mad, just like she's happy to see us here at all. "Mom's telling us about Texas."

Willa laughs. "Story time, huh?" Then she fits herself into the armchair, scrunching up her legs.

"What else?" I ask.

"Some of the homes are brick and stucco. Painted pink and cream and peach."

"Like sherbet?" I ask.

Willa laughs.

But Mom is serious. She understands. "Like sherbet. And the people are real nice. Friendly. Sometimes you'll be walking along and a stranger will just say hi."

I try to imagine people in Brooklyn looking up from their fast walks, arms swinging, saying hello to everyone who passed.

"Not like here," Willa says for me.

"Nope. If you said hi to everybody you saw here, you'd lose your voice," I say.

"Maybe so," Mom says. "But sometimes I think it would be nice."

"You could try it," I tell her.

"Maybe," she says, and she actually looks like she's thinking she might.

"Why'd you come to New York?" I ask. It's something I never even thought to wonder about until now.

"We both wanted an adventure," Willa says.

Mom nods. "Willa was the smart, practical one. I was the one with artsy dreams. New York City is the only place that could fit us both."

"Why don't you ever go back?" I ask Mom.

Something in her face falls like she forgot to catch it.

"It's expensive to travel," Willa reasons, echoing something I've heard Mom say before.

Mom nods. "Right." Then she says, "And without Meema there, there's no one left."

"No one?"

"No one who cares."

We're all quiet for a moment and I try not to think about the people who don't care about us. I think of tight-rope trees, of the river of Mom's hand, how Texas seemed to stretch from her heart to the tips of her fingers.

I wonder what New York City would become if I told it in a story, my hands a puppet show. Streets straight, like the cut of a knife. Rivers and oceans swirling around it all.

"I hope someday you get to see it," she tells me.

"Me too."

I reach the end of the clumpy braid I'm making. It doesn't look like Daddy's neat, smooth twist. Instead, it hangs from Mom's neck like a crooked tail.

"What's that?" Mom asks, and I watch her arm extend to my backpack. To the clear holder. To the bright yellow MetroCard.

I don't want to have to say what she already knows. My heart starts pumping inside me and I know I shouldn't have taken the money. We should have walked our skinny legs to school and back.

But I don't have to say anything because Willa answers for me. "A gift."

Mom stares at it. "How nice."

"I just thought that if they're going to be here, I'd like to do something. To make it easier," Willa says.

Mom rises up, her hair unspooling from the braid like yarn. "Then it's a good thing that we won't be here very long."

I squeeze into the corner of the couch, wishing I'd never taken the money, wishing we could just stay put for once.

Chapter 15

With Mom working a full day on Saturday, Willa takes us out first thing. "Who says you can't have cupcakes for breakfast?" she asks with a smile.

The cupcake shop is pink and tiled and the chairs are what Willa calls *old-timey,* with seat backs shaped like hearts.

Adare looks at the blackboard. The chalk writing tells us the names of the cupcakes, like Brooklyn Blackout and the Hummingbird. She sighs and pulls at my arm, then whines like she wants to leave. Her not wanting to be here makes me not want to be here, which makes me angry, because I really want to stay.

"Let's get a cupcake," Willa says sweetly, holding tight to Adare's wrist, and I decide to ignore her whining, hoping it'll just stop.

"I can't decide," I tell Willa.

"Hmm. What are you between?"

"The Flamingo"—I point at a cupcake with pink frosting clouds—"and this one." The other is swirled in chocolate.

"Only one solution."

"What?"

"We'll have to get them both."

Mom would tell me my eyes are bigger than my stomach, but she's not here and Willa is—and her *solution* sounds just right.

"Which would you like?" she asks Adare, who shrugs and tries squirming out of Willa's grasp.

"Just get her the same," I say.

We have to plop Adare down into a seat and she crosses her arms, kicks her legs against the metal, over and over, like this odd, tinging bell, while I pretend not to notice her fuss. When we get our cupcakes, I eat mine as fast as I can because I always feel like food's going to run out.

"Adare, you've barely touched yours."

Adare looks out the tall windows to the street, her arms still crossed. Her two little cupcakes sit like toadstools on a frilly-skirt plate.

With Adare lost in the world outside the window and Mom at work, I feel like it's a good time to start asking Willa all kinds of things without Mom giving me her sideways glare. "What's your fancy job?"

She laughs. "Corporate law."

"What's that?"

"It's hard to explain. It's boring. I work a lot. I should be working right now."

"How come you're not?"

"Because you're here." She smiles.

"Oh. But won't your boss get mad? Like Mom's, when she can't take a shift?"

"Oh, he will. He'll just be passive-aggressive about it."

I stare blankly.

"He'll pretend he's not mad, even though he is. Then he'll pat the heads of people who don't do nearly as much as I do. Right in front of me."

"Oh." I picture a suited old man, patting heads around the room like duck, duck, goose. "Do you have a boyfriend?" I ask.

Willa swallows her nibble of cupcake and shakes her head. "No boyfriend."

"How come?"

"I work too much. I don't have time for boyfriends." Then she glances down at the cupcake between her hands and picks at it, and I think Mom would probably tell me to quit my twenty-questions game.

I stare at the untouched cupcakes. "Adare, can I have yours?" When I look up, I hate what I see. Adare's holding on to her breath again.

"Let go," I say quietly.

"What'd you say?" Willa asks.

I shake my head like it's nothing, but with Adare it's always something, and Willa's too smart. She starts looking at Adare and stands up quick when she realizes what's going on. "Adare, honey. Stop that."

I should tell Willa she'll only make it worse by fussing over it, but as we watch Adare's face go pale, I know that even if she takes a breath, she'll hold it again. Once, at school, she did it thirty times in a half hour.

"Oh gosh. We should call someone, shouldn't we?" Willa swings around, like she's looking for someone to help.

Adare stares out the window, her face so still and so blank, it's like she'll fade away.

I watch her suck in air, then start over again. I don't say what I want to say: *Stop being who you are, stop ruining everything, just take a breath like the rest of us and move on.*

But she stays still. Every part of her is stuck and caught, like she's stunned, like she doesn't want to see anything, and I think about how she didn't want to be here and I knew it, but I didn't want to leave.

Willa pushes Adare's chair, sets her arms on her shoulders. "Stop that."

Another customer starts looking at us. "Is she all right?"

Willa looks toward me, like I should have the answer. "I don't know," I tell her, and she sighs and shakes her head.

Adare's face is so pale, I think I'll see through it to the

other side. Her eyes are two gray mirrors of glass, shining beneath the fluorescent lights of the cupcake shop.

More people are starting to look. I stand frozen, wishing and waiting for whatever it is that makes Adare want to do this to just release itself and let go.

Then she breathes out and in and her body comes unstuck.

I take my own breath in.

I tell Willa what I should have told her when we first came. "We should go. She doesn't want to be here."

Willa sets her hand on Adare's shoulder. "Oh, honey, oh, sweetie, you scared me."

Adare points toward the glass doors and is up, quick, running to them while Willa clutches her chest. "She does this often?" she asks me. "It can't be helped?"

I don't want to tell her the truth. Even if we've already showed up on her doorstep with our ratty old things and our skinny dumb cat, making scenes in cupcake shops, proving what she probably already knows—that we don't belong here with her, that we never will—I don't want to say what I know in my heart: *When it comes to Adare, nothing can be helped.*

I follow Adare into the fresh air, with the sound of cars in the distance, and the trees rustling, and the sidewalks ready for us to follow like a yellow-brick road.

Adare looks up to the sky, to the wing-flapping black that darts across it.

Willa steps up behind us, follows both of our gazes up. "What are you looking at?"

I watch the crows disappear and think how silly it would sound if I told her what I'm thinking. That they're ours. That they're off in the world without us and there's no one to keep their gifts at our old place on Hoyt Street while we're gone.

Chapter 16

On Monday, Mom insists on taking us to school on the subway, even though I tell her we're fine to walk. Willa went on and on about Adare's breath-holding, and even if Mom pretended it wasn't a big deal, I know it scared her. She says she misses taking us to school and I let her pretend that's why she won't let go of our hands.

She holds on as we loop through the turnstiles, keeping us close as we squeeze into the crowded subway car.

With each of us pressed against the silver gleaming pole, I think how quiet it is, how people lean into their papers, close their eyes, hide in their headphones. I catch the eye of one girl, whose hair is crisp black with green tips, as she bites her cracked nails, and I think of what Mom said about Texas. So I say, "Hello."

Her smile is crooked, sliding up to just one side. "Hey."

Mom holds on to my shoulders, curls around me, dips her hair at my chest. "Someone's friendly today."

I nod. "Yup. Like in Texas."

When we come up from underground, the sky is less blue than when we last saw it, and the air is cold, like it's backing away from spring. We drop Adare off first, so it's just me and Mom. She holds tight to my hand and I feel a talk coming on.

"You can't say hello to strangers," she tells me.

"Why not?"

"It's not safe."

"It's friendly," I argue.

She shakes her head. "Sometimes *friendly* is an invitation for someone to do something they shouldn't."

"Like Franklin?" I ask.

"Like that."

I remember the blank hallways of Ennis House, Old Lou on the stairs, like always, and Franklin, who was just a few years older than me, tall and skinny, the kind of kid who walked slow and never really said anything, whose blue eyes always looked so big and lost and scared, being taken away by the police. Yelling echoed through the hallways, with his mom shouting, tears rolling down her cheeks, saying he was *just a boy* and then choking on her words, so nothing made sense.

When I asked Mom what had happened, she said, "He did something he shouldn't."

When I asked Fred C., he told it plain. "He's dealing."

I couldn't imagine Franklin selling drugs. I'd passed him a hundred times on the steps or standing outside, leaning up against the scaffolding, looking out into the street like he was just wishing and waiting for something new.

Once, I stopped to make a note about a skinny pin oak and he asked me what I was doing, but Mom snatched me away before I could answer.

If I had answered, if I had told him, I wonder if that would've been an *invitation*.

"I just need you to be careful, Cora," she tells me.

"I am," I say.

"I know. I know." She says it twice, like she's the one who needs convincing.

We stop in front of the school's entrance, but Mom does not let go of my hand. "I know this has been hard on you, Cora. The break-in. Holing up at Willa's. It's different for your sister. An advantage of being Adare is she doesn't get uprooted the way you do." Her hand clutches mine. "But I promise. We'll find a place to be."

I want to believe her, but I can't. I'm starting to believe there's no place we belong. I rip my hand away before she can say another word, then I rush up the steps to school.

Chapter 17

At lunch, I sit in the schoolyard with my Tree Book, the cold concrete against my pink checkered skirt.

Sabina marches up to me and starts setting up hula hoops. "Let's play jump the river," she says, like we do it every day.

I don't know the game, but I want to sound like I do. "You start," I say.

Sabina rolls a pink hoop and lets it flop to the ground.

Then she sets the rest of them in a pattern of lily pads and jumps between them. Her focus is so sharp, I can imagine the water rushing around her toes in a swirl.

"Babies," a voice calls out.

Sabina looks up from inside her hoop. Meredith Crane parades past, her friends cascading behind her like a frilly gown draping the floor. I stay seated. I'm not even playing

Sabina's baby game, but Meredith blows her bangs up and juts her chin out at me.

"So, Cora, I hear you're getting sent to math class with the retarded kids, like your sister."

Everything inside me goes blank. I know the word isn't right, but I don't know what to say back. "I don't . . . They're not . . . ," I start, but I can't find the words to say it right without it being wrong. *I'm* not like *them. They're* not like *them. I'm* not like *her.* Like Adare. *Wrong.*

"*Cretins!*" Sabina shouts.

I swing my head to Sabina, wondering what in the world she's doing saying something like that, and Meredith stops in her tracks, her back to us, hands on hips, shoulders in a rise and fall. When she turns, she sticks out her lower lip, blows her bangs up in a parachute puff. "What'd you call me, Griffin?"

"Look it up, *Crane.*"

Meredith marches over, takes her foot—sequined shiny in a pink ballet flat—and slams it at the edge of the hoop. It flips up, nearly smacking Sabina in the chin.

Sabina stands still. Her eyelashes drop to her cheeks and she closes her eyes, breathes deep, then lets her breath go, air whistling through her teeth like water through a straw.

I watch Meredith shift her jaw, confused. Then she mutters under her breath, "Freak."

"Meredith . . . ," I say, heat rushing to my cheeks, my head shaking back and forth, waiting for the right words to come. But something about the way Sabina stands, sturdy and sure, makes me feel weak, the kind of girl who doesn't know how to defend her sister or herself and who pees in her pants in the middle of the night. So my voice is barely a whisper when I say, "Just leave us alone."

Meredith squawks out a laugh and sends her bangs flying up again.

Sabina doesn't move.

We stand like this. Sabina, a narrow stalk. Meredith and her twisted jaw. Me, tucked next to a line of hoops with the wind passing through.

I want to be done with Meredith, with *this*, with *me* not knowing how to say what I should.

And like she knows, like she hears my head whirling, Sabina grabs my arm and we pinwheel across the schoolyard as fast as we can, leaving Meredith gaping behind. When we reach the opposite end of the fence, my chest heaving, I say, "Thanks."

A glint of sun crosses Sabina, who shrugs. "What's wrong with your sister anyway?"

I look into her big eyes and it doesn't seem like she's being mean, only wondering. I don't know how to answer because I don't know, either. "Nothing. She's what people call *special*," I say, repeating the word I've heard all my life.

"Special." It's like she's rolling the word around her

tongue. "It comes from the word *species,* you know. Every-one's special." But she says it like *spee-cial.* "We're human. We have all the same parts. Well, I mean, except, like, boys and stuff."

"Oh," I say. "Then I guess Adare's parts work differently."

She rolls her eyes and laughs. "All of our parts work differently. Right?"

"Right."

She unfurls her fingers and places her palm in front of mine. Inside sits a bottle-cap necklace stamped with a purple star.

"What's that?" I ask.

"I found it," she says. "You can have it, if you want."

"But where'd it come from?"

"When you're looking for things, you find things." She places her hand around mine and drops the necklace in my palm with a smile.

The bell sings out and Sabina turns quick, then stops herself to look back at me. "Oh, I almost forgot. I found something of yours. Come find me later." Then she loses herself in the fast squeeze of kids lining up to get inside.

Chapter 18

All afternoon, I think about Sabina and her pinwheeling me across the schoolyard, how she pokes at my Tree Book and collects words. I slap my locker closed after school, wondering what she's got of mine. I mean, what's mine to have anyway? Something in me wonders if it's the broken greenhouse or one of a million things we've left behind, moving from place to place all these years.

I scan the hallway and hear her squeaking toward the exit. She marches a foot taller than everyone else through the halls.

I run after her, nudge her bony shoulder. "So what is it?"

She swings around, her winter coat still bunched across her tall-drink, skinny frame. "You wanna see?"

"Of course."

"I gotta take you," she says, and tucks her books underneath her arm and starts skidding away.

"Where?" I try to keep up.

"Over by Miss Li's. It's only, like, ten minutes from here."

I know I should be studying for tomorrow's algebra test, but I also want to know what it is. "I've got to get my sister," I tell her. "I can't just go off."

"Okay, then. You lead. But you gotta be quick. I've got snack time. Then homework to take care of."

She pushes out the doors and the sun is at us, light barreling across the concrete, the air creeping toward spring. I look up at the buds on my schoolyard cherry blossom. I hold on to its green whispers. A picture in my mind. I'll have to make a note in my Tree Book later.

We walk the two blocks to Adare's school, only sort of together, because Sabina stays behind me, boots burping across the sidewalk in their sticky hum. I wonder why she doesn't get regular shoes instead of these huge moon boots, but I don't say a thing, just swing my arms, trying to figure out what I'm getting myself into.

"Can't you just tell me what it is?" I ask.

"Nuh-uh. I've gotta make sure it's there."

"Can't you just bring it tomorrow?"

She sighs, like I'm asking all the wrong questions. "No can do."

"Don't you have to get home?" I ask.

"Don't you?"

"Eventually."

Adare sits on the steps, like always, looking up into the sky. It makes me look up at the way the clouds wisp and I hold on to another picture for my Tree Book. I think I'll make a note of an afternoon sky: a quick line swish to paint the day.

She smiles when she sees me and then her eyes mirror Sabina behind me, curious and having to know. "Hi," she says fast and bright.

Sabina doesn't startle, like some people do. She just says hi right back.

I swing my arm out to present her. "This is Sabina."

Adare's smile softens and she waves, and as she jumps from one step to the next, I remember the last time Sabina saw her, shoes off, hair tangled, sitting on Miss Li's filthy floor.

"We're going on a walk," I tell her.

Adare takes my hand and I say a quick prayer in my head that her shoes stay on.

"*You* lead," I tell Sabina.

"I think you're gonna like this." Then she shuffles ahead.

We take Smith Street. I scan trees. Lots of honey locusts and pin oaks, and blocks with no trees at all.

Sabina switches arms, crushes her books against her

side. I watch how she keeps her eyes on the ground, braids slipping to her nose, staying close to the fence the way she did the other day after school.

"Don't your arms get tired from all the books?" I ask.

"Not really. This way I just have what I need. Don't your shoulders hurt with that backpack?"

"Sometimes," I admit.

Her stride is big and she takes us to the Ninth Street Bridge. The subway sneaks above us. The canal water sits in its stink below. I look into it. There's a reflection of blue sky that melts into the murky brown sludge. The junkyard sits with piles of scrap metal in giant heaps. The arm of the crane is stretched out and frozen.

I think we're going straight toward Miss Li's, but she turns toward the canal and slips along the gray branches of old bushes and logs.

I stop. "Are we allowed over here?"

She doesn't look back. Just marches ahead. "Of course."

I hold tight to Adare, look around, and see there's nobody here. There's the little dip of a stone wall toward the water, and a stretching plank of mud and grass next to the junkyard.

"How far is it?" I ask.

"Just up there," she calls back, pointing toward a red warehouse and a big, old tree whose roots dig deep into the mud.

"Come on." I lead Adare along the narrow path. The

smell of the canal is wet and sweet, sticking to the air all gummy.

We walk along the edge of the canal, beside a metal barrier. The rocks slip to the water and we keep our feet on the dirt. Tall grass juts out, hanging over the dirt like it can't hold itself up.

Before I can wonder what might be mine, what she wants to show me, the gray and silver and brown of everything here lights up Adare's eyes. She rips her hand from mine and sinks to the wet ground.

I can't believe what I'm seeing.

It's the charcoal cat. His eyes are caught somewhere between blue and yellow, a leafy emerald green.

"You found him," I say to Sabina.

"More like he found me."

"That's amazing. How'd you remember him?"

"Just did," she says.

"Does he come here every day?" I ask.

"Yup. Isn't he sweet?"

"I promised Adare I'd find him," I tell her. "I thought it was a dumb promise."

"Guess it worked out." She smiles.

Adare strokes the cat, who isn't scared like he was at Miss Li's. He stretches out. A ball of fur beneath a sun that feels like it's trying to hang on longer to the day.

I look around. There are empty tuna fish cans, damp

cardboard, and a broken picture frame, its glass cut out in puzzle shapes.

At the edge of the warehouse, there's a fallen tree trunk. It rests in a drawn-out line, all hollow and wet from old rain. Next to it stands a big, sturdy tree. Fifty, sixty feet, maybe. Tall and straight, with the wind tossing all the leafless stems.

I move toward it. The bark is a twist of gray and brown, running lines that sweep up and up. I can't believe what I think I'm seeing.

I throw my backpack to the ground, rip it open, and grab my Tree Book. I flip the pages to a photograph of the tree of heaven.

I match the two barks. Both their bumps are scattered in the shape of broken diamonds.

"The tree of heaven," I whisper.

"What?" Sabina asks.

I speak up. "The tree of heaven."

"So?"

"This . . . is my dad's tree," I tell her. "He studied it for a long time. I think this is it."

I make sure I've got it right.

I look at the polluted canal. A tree that can grow in the worst conditions. I study the photograph again, placing all of us here. Daddy, the photograph, the tree, me. And that's when I match the fallen tree beside us. There's even a tip of the red warehouse in the corner. All of it's right there in the photo and right next to me.

My heart beats fast.

"This is it," I say. "For sure."

Beneath the tree it's cooler and darker. The empty spaces between branches carve out broken pieces of sky. I feel my feet in the dirt, imagining Daddy right here the day he died. Then I imagine myself inside the tree.

I want to get up in it.

I study the branches. The first nook for my foot is way too high. Even if I hug my legs and arms around it to get up, it'd scrape my wrists and hands.

I move closer, trying to figure it out. A ladder would help. Or a rope. I stand against the rough column of its bark. The roots don't Halloween-crawl out like some of the other trees. They are buried deep. If I look up, I stand beneath a crown of bending arms, reaching around one another.

"So this is where I keep everything," Sabina tells me.

I'd almost forgotten she was there.

I open my eyes quick. "Keep what?"

While Adare strokes the charcoal cat, Sabina crouches to the ground and points into the hollow of the fallen tree. I kneel beside her and look in. Nestled inside the bark are neat stacks of crumpled paper.

"What are they?"

"Grocery lists. Letters. Doodles. Once I found this postcard that was all old-school, about riding roller coasters at Coney Island. It was signed *Miss Grayson*. Like she was somebody's neighbor or teacher or something. Look at this." She grabs from one stack and holds out a wrinkled yellow paper. "A love letter."

I look it over. *Dear Karen,* in wild, looping script.

"I found it on top of the garbage, next to a broken photo frame. Someone's breakup. Don't you think?"

"I guess." I look at all the tidy stacks. "Why do you keep them?"

"They're somebody's memories."

"Why here? They could get all wet and ruined."

"I've got too many boxes filled up at home. I've been collecting notes for years. You'd be surprised what people lose."

I run my fingers over the letter. *Dear Karen, There's so much I wasn't able to say.*

There's a rustle in the water and it startles both of us. We stand up quick. I look across the canal at a string of three houseboats. A boy sits in a wooden canoe with a skinny pole slipping into the water. His hair is a big, wild nest above his head.

"My brother."

"Brother? When you said you live on the canal, you actually meant *on* it?"

"Yup. In that houseboat, just over there." Her hand stretches out to the white boat across the narrow water.

I've heard of people living on houseboats but never met anyone who did.

The boy stops in the middle of the canal.

"Should we go?" I ask.

"Nah. He's just shy."

Adare rests her head against the fallen tree. Her arms curl around the charcoal cat, stroking his fur. I know she's not going anywhere.

The wind crawls over us. There's the steady whish of the expressway and a siren calling, far away. The boy's paddle slips through the water and Adare lifts the cat to her lap. She stands up slow, stroking and shushing him, the way she does with Sookie.

The canoe slaps against a lopsided dock, and he ties a busted-up rope to anchor it.

His thick, wild hair is like something from a fairy tale. The fading blue sky matches the blaze of his eyes, and he wears an oversize hoodie over swishy pants and the same tall rubber boots as his sister.

Sabina extends her arm, like she's taking a bow. "You can show them, if you want."

He's cautious. He walks to the far end of the dock. Then onto the grass. Then he marches to us. Sabina ruffles his hair as he plunges quickly to the ground, resting on his stomach, peering into the hollowed-out tree.

He jumps back to his feet and places his finger over his lips to hush me. The other hand bows out toward the black yawning trunk, like he's telling me to look.

I walk over and kneel on the damp grass. The scratchy tufts gnaw at my hands. Then I peer in, looking real close. I piece together an image inside the dark cavity. Soft matching feathers, folded napkin-neat. And two huge yellow-swamped eyes staring back at me.

I place my hands in the grass, careful not to say a word, staring at this no-necked bird with cat ears.

It's quiet and knowing and not quite scared, just tucked away, like it found the only place in the world it belongs. I stare into its eyes and wonder how it came to be right here.

Then I stand up and whisper, "What is it?"

"A screech owl," the boy says.

"Where'd it come from?"

He shakes his head. He looks like some kind of forest creature, tangled and messy.

"This is Jacob," Sabina tells me.

"I'm Cora," I say. "And this is Adare—"

"Hi—" Adare says at the exact same time.

Jacob is confused at her friendliness and doesn't say anything back. He marches past the screech owl toward Adare and the cat. He clicks his tongue a few times. "Come 'ere."

The cat's loving and nestling against Adare's legs, looping through her bent elbow.

Jacob scoops the cat in his arms and folds him against his chest.

Adare smiles at the cat. She runs her fingers across his back one more time, not worrying about the boy's protective hug. "I love him," she says, the same way she told me the night we escaped Miss Li's, as if it's the simple truth.

"You can have him," Sabina says.

Adare's eyes grow big.

"No, she can't," Jacob chimes in, real fast.

I watch Adare's hand stay rooted on the cat's humped-up spine. Jacob doesn't know that Adare's got a way with cats. If Adare wanted him, he'd be hers.

"I love him," she says again.

I look around—at the tree of heaven and the way the ground slopes so that the trunk leans over the canal. It was *here* that Sabina found him and led us. To Daddy's tree. And I don't want to disturb a thing. I shake my head, firm. "No. He belongs here." I turn to Jacob, wondering out loud, "Do you go to Adare's school?"

"No."

"Jacob does homeschool on the boat," Sabina tells me. "After years of whining about it, I finally got my dad to let me go to a real school. He thinks it shows *self-reliance*."

Suddenly, it makes sense how Sabina walks around without caring what anyone thinks of her, plays weird games like jump the river, talks back to Meredith, and never carries a schoolbag. She doesn't know a thing about school.

"It's snack time," Jacob reminds her.

"I know." Then she turns to me. "Wanna come over for a snack?"

Jacob doesn't look up to hear my answer. Instead, he glares at Sabina, who says, "What?" Then she turns to me. "You don't have to come, but you can."

I look at the tree of heaven like I've finally got closer to Daddy again. Now all I have to do is figure out a way to get in it. But I feel my empty stomach, and even if I know an entire pantry's waiting at Willa's, I can't seem to say no to food. Not ever. "We'll come."

Sabina smiles.

Jacob runs to the canoe, loosening the rope and tossing it back to the dock.

We follow him there. The cat leaps along, his little legs balancing on the wooden seat planks.

Chapter 19

We cross the canal, leaving the screech owl and its wide eyes creeping. This is the closest I've ever been to the canal water, which is army green and still, like a big, flat tarp, all spread out. There's a rainbow swirl of oil and soap foam. Garbage sits tangled in brushwood that barely moves, even as Sabina paddles.

"Don't touch the water," she warns us.

I wouldn't want to. Even Adare, who doesn't usually follow rules, keeps her hands buried in her lap as we float across to the opposite dock.

"This guy keeps swimming in the canal, to prove it's okay or whatever," Sabina tells us. "It's like some activist thing. But I'm pretty sure he's going to be a mutant some-day. I mean, right? Seriously."

Their houseboat is big but narrow and it noses out in

front. There's a series of overgrown plants dangling from the awning over the entrance. I wonder how they grow on a boat that could take off and sail away.

Jacob doesn't say much, just stares a lot at me and Adare, but Sabina leads us like she's a tour guide. "The back, here, is called the *stern*. Left is *port*. Right is *starboard*. You have to know that if you want to sail because that's how people say it and you don't want to look like you don't know what you're doing. You get to the cabin from this little door right here." She points as we walk the tiny deck, our shoes flapping against the wood panels, and then she shoves it open.

Jacob goes in and says, "Look, Mom. Sabina's got friends."

He says it not like he's announcing we're here but like he's announcing our relationship to Sabina. Like it might be a big deal that she has *friends*. I wonder if we can be called that. She saved me from Meredith, gave me the bottle-cap necklace, and brought me here. But when I look at her, her face has nothing written on it for me to know.

I grab tight to Adare's hand and we duck our heads so they don't bump the top of the door. We stay bent and crunched as we walk the narrow steps. I'm surprised— when we reach the cabin, it looks less like a boat and more like a house, with curtains tied with ribbons along the tiny windows, and there's the littlest kitchen. All the utensils and pots and pans hang from colorful hooks along the wood walls. There's even a flowered teapot on a burner and cups and plates stacked neat in a metal rack.

We stand on a series of rugs woven of blue and burgundy and green straw. They're circling the floor like Olympic rings. There's a sitting chair with an afghan and throw pillows, and four bunks, two on each side. They're folded up against the wall, so when you pull them down, they become real beds to sleep on. They have something like them in the bed and bath department at Mom's store. *Murphy beds,* she calls them, and she always says with this sad kind of look in her eye that they're perfect for even the tiniest spaces in Brooklyn.

Mrs. Griffin stands at the sink, washing dishes, and when Adare says "Hi," she turns around. She's tall, like Sabina. The frizz of her hair grazes the slanting roof of the cabin.

"Well, hello," she says back.

"This is Cora and Adare," Sabina says. She reaches up to a shelf stuffed with jars and boxes—like Willa's pantry, only Willa's is organized by size and type and this is a mixed-up jumble. She pulls out a box, opens it, and hands over a sleeve of graham crackers. "Cinnamon," she clarifies, and I think again of Meema as I rip open the package and slip the crisp squares out.

Mrs. Griffin sets a dishrag at her hip, looks between

me and Adare, and smiles, easy-like. She extends her arms, talks with a big laugh in her voice, "Welcome to our humble abode."

"This place is so—"

"Tiny," Sabina interrupts.

"I was going to say *cool*."

"We live *untethered*," Sabina says. "The electricity runs on the sun. And we collect rainwater through a filtration system Dad set up on the deck. We're tied to nothing. Nobody."

"I like that." It sounds like a way of living that Mom would like, too. I think how nice it would be to have the same home no matter where you are.

Then Mrs. Griffin spins to a clock on the wall. "Almost homework time," she announces, and her eyebrow flips up with a warning. "We run a tight ship around here." Again, with a laugh, like it's always bubbling up inside her and she can't help but let it slip out. She turns to me and Adare. "You're welcome to stay."

"We've got a timer and everything." Sabina holds up an egg timer and rolls her eyes.

"Don't want to overcook." Mrs. Griffin laughs.

It'd be nice to sit cozied up beneath the low roof, working through assignments. But I think of Adare. I imagine trying to have her sit still with her to-do lists and her sighs, her refusals and whines. I don't think that would work inside Mrs. Griffin's tight ship. That's probably not what she thinks of as homework time.

"We can't. We've got to . . ." I pause, not sure. ". . . get back."

"I'm sure you've got your own homework rules at your house," Mrs. Griffin says.

"Right." I nod, fast, because there's something about Mrs. Griffin, no matter how soft her laugh, like you'd better have answers, like you'd better not dillydally.

"You live in Gowanus?" she asks.

"We used to."

"Rough around the edges here, huh?"

"I guess, but . . ." She waits for me to say more, like she's interested in what I've got to say. And something makes me feel like I can explain. "I like it. It's kind of—I don't know—on its way. To getting better."

"*On its way.*" She thinks it over, like she's tasting the idea on her tongue. Then she winks real fast. "I like that."

"Thank you for the graham crackers." I hold up the crinkling pack.

"Anytime." Mrs. Griffin smiles wide.

And even if I want to stay here forever, I look at Jacob, who stands gnawing on graham crackers, looking at my sister. She shoves the crackers in her mouth, crumbs sticking to the creases of her lips as she stares at a set of hanging crystal chimes.

I take hold of Adare's wrist, but she doesn't budge,

stays flat-footed, reaching one arm out to the chimes. I pull at her, but she rips her arm from me.

"Adare, we have to go."

Adare stomps and whines and sounds like the kind of person I don't want her to be. The slow kid people like Meredith make fun of.

I pull her out of the boat and away.

Sometimes I wish Adare could be invisible.

Sabina stands on the dock with her hands in her pocket. "Sorry."

"For what?" I ask.

"You must think we're totally weird homeschooling crazies."

I laugh. "No."

"Snack time. And egg timers for homework. We even have a reading hour before bed." She smacks her head. "Ugh. I just told you we have a reading hour. Sorry."

I want to tell Sabina to stop sorrying, because it sounds nice, having snack time and a reading hour and knowing you've always got to be somewhere doing what you need to do. "I like your place," I tell her. "Your mom's cool."

"Cool? Well, let's not go that far." She lingers on the dock. "You guys can come back to see the screech owl. And the cat. I mean, if you want," she says.

"I want to," I say.

"Good."

And I think this means we're friends. "I'll see you in

math tomorrow," I tell her. And I remember the test, let the dread of it sink into me.

But before I go, I look back at the houseboat and, on the other side of the canal, at the tree of heaven.

I've found Daddy's favorite tree.

Chapter 20

We're only three stops from Willa's place, and I sit on the subway train, facing into the car, while Adare kneels backward on the seat, her nose pressed against the window. Strips of light scan her face, the way the chimes did, and I watch her reflection. Her shape sways and shifts with the train.

I map everything in my Tree Book—the cherry blossom at school, the sky above Adare while she waited at the steps, the brushwood in the canal, and the flowers hanging from Sabina's houseboat. Then I sketch the tree of heaven, whose trunk I draw to the edge of one page but whose branches disappear past it into the wide-open space of the subway, through the windows, out the tunnel, and back into Brooklyn, where it started.

Then I close the book and hold it at my chest.

I wonder how I'll tell Mom all we saw. I sift through

my bag for an inky pen and press it to my palm, trying to steady it against the bump of the train. I draw the eyes of an owl and flap my fingers over its gaze.

But it turns out Mom's not back yet. It's Willa who stands with her elbows slumped at the kitchen counter and shoots up like a daffodil when we toss the door open.

"There you are." It surprises me. She says it like she has some kind of stake in us, like we're hers. She eyes my muddy sneakers. "Where have you been?"

"Nowhere," I say quickly, letting the lie drip out. The tree feels like a secret no one else can know.

She folds her arms, as if she can't decide whether to believe me, and I know we don't belong here. Not with Willa, who stands as tall as her windows, who has stacks of pillows and sheets in neat folds, whose fridge is always full, and whose view of the sky, behind her, spreading along the wraparound glass, is bigger than any I've known.

For a moment, I wonder if I can tell her the truth. Then I think of the empty warehouses and the strays and the lingering old houseboats and know that Willa won't like that even a little. If I want to go back—and I *have* to go back—there's no way she can know.

"Do you like staying here?" she asks, like she can read my mind.

I'm about to nod, flap my mouth about the cupcake shop and the snack fridge. But I stop myself, fast.

I don't know how to answer Willa with her folded arms

and her long legs, ankles crossed over each other, one foot tapping out her question. It's something Mom asks when we end up somewhere new. *Do you like it here?* And I never answer straightaway. I look to see Mom's face. I look to see if *she* thinks we should go or stay.

I can always tell whether Mom can picture us in a place. I watch how she circles it, walks it. Whether she takes her hair from her face, giving her pink cheeks air, or leaves it hanging limp down her back. I can tell how she sees us inside the four walls. And once I know, I follow real quick with the same answer.

But Mom's not here. And the starched apron on the wall is splattered with *frijoles charros*. Our ugly patchwork quilt stretches across Willa's stiff white couch. There's a brown smudge on the cushion from Adare's filthy feet. There's no way Willa wants us to stay.

"I dunno," I say with a shrug, like I don't care—when really, if it were up to me, I'd stay here forever and a day.

"Because you can, Cora. You know that. Don't you?"

I watch her eyes and they don't skid around the room, the way Mom's caseworker, Tilda's, sometimes do, like she's about to tell us the kind of story we want to hear, the kind she later rips away. "We can?"

"Your mother and I have known each other a long time," she says. "I mean, look at this place." She swirls around. "What's the point in having it if you're going to be all alone?"

I look at it. So white and empty. She doesn't have beanbag chairs or greenhouses or beet-stained curtains dripping to the floor.

"You *have* to stay." She smiles.

And even though I know I shouldn't, I let myself believe we will.

Then Willa unfolds her arms and says, "Now, *what* shall we order for dinner?" She makes her way to the menu drawer, sliding takeout menus between her fingers. "I don't feel like Thai, not tonight. Do you?"

"Not tonight," I agree because I'd agree with anything Willa said if it meant we could stay between her bare white walls, settling at the edges of her memories, getting closer and closer to this place she calls home.

Chapter 21

That night, I sit at one end of the couch and Adare sits at the other. We bunch our knees up and match our feet while Sookie warms our toes. I hear the murmur of Mom and Willa's easy conversation from Willa's room and I sit with algebra and my Tree Book in my lap.

I should be studying for tomorrow's big exam, but instead I draw the spring's first leaves into the book's pages.

"I'm gonna climb it," I say out loud. I don't even know if she's listening, if the thoughts that are falling from my head and twisting out my tongue make any sense to her.

"Specially when it flowers," I continue.

"Okay," Adare agrees.

She sits with her butterfly wings sticking out from the quilt. She's worn them so long, the glitter's gone gray across the faded pink. They used to be mine until I decided real living things were more interesting than pretend ones.

The sky is dark and full along the huge wraparound windows, and with the city and the bridge lit, it feels kind of like we're floating across it. Like the floor disappeared and, with Adare's wings and the branches of my Tree Book growing and growing, we're lost in the swirl.

I close my eyes and feel us weightless.

Then I hear Mom's voice rise from Willa's room. The walls are a thin paper sheet. "Don't start, Willa."

Willa's voice withers and swells.

Mom's voice is even. "It's none of your business."

"They do as they please," Willa says, and I wonder, *Who does as they please? Us?*

Mom says something I can't make out, but Willa's voice is big now. "And Adare—she needs more than you can give her."

"She has what she needs."

Willa's voice is a rolling roar. "How much longer can you live like this?"

But the conversation is done. Mom's left the room. Adare straightens up and her wings catch the sparkling lights from the city. I turn over onto the book and press my head into the couch, like I've been sleeping, like I haven't heard a thing.

I hear Mom at the closet where Willa stacks the pillows and the sheets. There's some rummaging, but my nose is smashed into the scratchy white of the couch, breathing new-furniture smell and the warmth of my own body. I keep my head stuffed there, my arm wrapped around the book's smooth cover. I can still feel the glow of the city through the glass. It stays trapped behind my eyelids, jumping in fizzing light patterns.

So Willa thinks we're wild and set loose in Brooklyn. She thinks Adare hasn't been given what she *needs*. What does she need? Something special. Those are Adare's needs. I imagine Sabina sounding it out like *species—spee-cial*.

I trap my book tighter and tighter against my chest, and my hand goes numb. The owl on my palm is crushed.

I hear Mom, closer now, at the wide white matching chair. She breathes in like she has to blow her nose. She breathes in like she no longer can.

Chapter 22

At math the next day, Sabina slides into class with a big old grin at me and I try to smile back, even if everything in me is sinking.

I don't want to take this test.

But I don't have a choice. I sign my name in pencil at the top. I run an eraser across the page to see the pink dust swirl, and then I brush it away. The rubber pieces stick to the cold desk. I knock my worn sneakers on the metal bar.

What is the multiplicative inverse of ½?

Nothing inside me knows. I don't have a string of numbers in me waiting to get out. I only have Mom's painting genes and the pictures caught in my palms. What good are they when you need real answers, a solid number written in no. 2 pencil?

I glance up at Mrs. Belz, who sits at her desk, her nose

pointing out at us all. We catch eyes and she's got this look like she's disappointed in me before she needs to be.

What is the multiplicative inverse of ½?

I look toward the window, but Mrs. Belz has shut the blinds. I wish I was in art class with Mrs. Folaris and her funky outfits and her soft voice.

I run my hand across the printed questions, my fingernails like rounded moons. I let my pencil trace the night sky of the page and draw ten fingernail moons.

Before I know it, I've placed a tree beneath each one. Sticks of prickled pine trees go soft in my imagination. I build a row of crows' nests because crows like to build their homes in evergreens—trees that never lose their leaves. Permanent, no matter how cold. Not like most plants, which have to regrow them each year.

I let time disappear, and when Mrs. Belz asks us to place our pencils down, my pencil is a dull nub.

She collects the tests, her heels pattering the floor like an easy rain, and when she comes to me, she looks down at the gray shadows of my drawing. It fills the entire page and the spaces where the answers should be.

"Miss Quinn. Would you like to keep that?"

I nod.

There are no numbers in me. Only pictures. And a stubborn snap of Adare that's being sent straight to remedial math.

Chapter 23

At lunch, Sabina and I lie out on the concrete, the sun beating down on us. Instead of jumping the river, it's like we're floating right in it.

"I didn't know any of the answers," I tell her, stabbing my fist on the pavement. "Is math easy for you?" I ask.

"Uh-huh."

"Why?"

"I'm just good at numbers."

"My dad was good at numbers," I say. "Not me."

"You'll catch up."

I don't tell her about remedial math. I don't tell her that catching up is no longer possible for me. "Why in the world did you ever want to come to school, Sabina?" I ask, because I've got to know why anyone would subject herself to this.

"I know it doesn't make much sense with all the moving we do, if we're just going to the next place and the next one. But it was just like, I've got to start *being* somewhere. For real. Ya know?"

"You never made any friends?"

"I don't know. Not the kind of friends you sit with looking at clouds."

"Looking at clouds? That's what being friends is all about?"

"Yeah."

"You read too many love notes," I tell her.

She laughs. "What's it about, then?"

"It's . . ." I think about this really hard. I think about how I don't usually talk to anybody because I'm afraid we'll up and go. I think of Mom and Willa, after all these years. I don't want to say the wrong thing, so I just say, "I don't know."

"Well, I think it's chatting and looking up at clouds," she says firmly.

I smile and look up. "How long have you lived on the houseboat?" I ask.

"Forever."

"Do you get seasick?" I wonder.

"Nope."

"How many places have you lived?"

"A million," she says.

"Me too."

"But, then, it's kind of like just one. We're always on the boat."

So she hasn't had to leave roaches and an Old Lou on the stairs or go to another new placement with no bathroom.

"Don't you want to quit leaving?"

"I don't know. Leaving a place is easy when you haven't really left anything behind."

"Mmm," I say. "I get that." Then I tell her what I haven't told anyone, not ever. "Technically, we're homeless."

I can't see her reaction, not while we're looking up at the sky, and I think maybe I get why looking at clouds is necessary to a friendship. Maybe you need to not see what the other person really thinks. Maybe you just hope for the best.

But I feel her beside me and she doesn't move. "You live on the street?" she asks.

I shake my head. "It's not like that. We don't have our own place. We did when my dad was alive, and then there was this place on Hoyt Street, but then . . . we just didn't anymore."

While I'm looking up, I guess Sabina's looking down. She rolls over to her side and I shift my gaze, watch her take hold of an old-looking rag of paper. She sits up fast and unfolds the neat square. I sit up with her.

"What is it?"

Her eyes scan the lined notebook page. "Probably somebody passing a note in class." She frowns. "It's wet." She hands the paper to me.

"*Dear Becca,*" I read. Then I look over the ruined blue ink. I can only make out some of the note. The beginning of one sentence, the end of another. It's all blobbed and smeared.

I turn to the back. Sabina reads over my shoulder at the bottom of the page, "*Your former friend, Jen.*"

She looks closer. "*Jess,*" she corrects herself. "You know a Jess?"

I shake my head. "You know a Becca?"

"Nope." Sabina takes the note from me, folds it back up into a neat little square. "*Former friend.* Bummer."

"Bummer," I repeat.

Sabina stuffs the note in the pocket of her puff skirt and leans her head back on her hands.

"What do you think happened?"

I shift back to the sky, too. "Could be a million things."

"It had to be bad—to write a long note like that."

"She probably called her out for being a jerk or something."

"Who?"

"Becca."

"Called Jess out?"

"The other way around."

"Mmm." She thinks it over. "I bet Becca didn't lose the note. I bet she threw it away."

"Could be a million things," I say again.

"We'll never know."

I look up, trying to forget about Becca and Jess, not wanting to think about the million ways a friendship can fall apart.

Sabina twirls a braid around her fingers. "My dad's a fisherman, so we lived on the Chesapeake Bay once for a whole year," she tells me. "There was this humungous houseboat community, near a school and everything. I used to watch the kids play. They'd set out hula hoops and stuff. And jump in them. I kept trying to figure out how to play, just by watching. I made up the name—jump the river. But I don't even know the real rules."

I remember Sabina setting out her hula hoops the other day, how it felt like she knew exactly what she was doing. I guess she didn't.

"Staying in one place can be nice," she says. "But it's nothing like living in the world."

Sitting here, looking up at the huge sky, I want to tell her what I know: that the world is too big and you have to find your piece of it if you want to survive.

Chapter 24

When we get to Willa's place, I'm carrying two pieces of paper. The crumpled math test with a set of moons and a folded-up note from Mrs. Belz about me switching to remedial math—after I insisted we didn't have a phone number for her to call.

Willa jumps from the couch when we open the door and her smile is almost too wide, like it's got this kind of knowing inside it. "I'm glad you're back. We have a visitor today."

"A visitor?" It sounds so proper.

"A friend. From school."

School? I imagine Mrs. Belz slapping the elevator buttons, stomping down Willa's hallway to me.

"From *my* school?" I ask while Adare runs to the refrigerator and grabs a jar of peanut butter. I lean over her, taking out some plastic-wrapped string cheese.

"From *my* old school. College. I thought she might like to meet you and Adare."

"What for?" I pull a strand of rubbery cheese.

Then I hear the toilet flush and the bathroom door opens and a woman walks into the hall, her flowered skirt swishing over flats that look too small for her swollen feet. She wears a big beaded necklace with a giant purple stone that rests on her puffy chest.

"This is Jade."

She reaches her hand out. "Is this Adare?"

I shake my head. "Cora."

She nods and looks over at Adare, who has her nose pressed up against the window.

"She's just as tall as me," I say, like it matters, her knowing that we could be the same if Adare breathed right when she was born.

"It's funny, isn't it, when little sisters catch up?"

"I guess."

"My littlest sister towers over me."

"Come here, Adare," Willa calls out, singsong.

"What grade are you in?" Jade asks me.

"Seventh."

"Almost there."

"Where?" I ask.

"High school."

"Cora's in advanced classes," Willa chimes in.

"Smart girl."

I think of the note folded in the pocket of my beet-purple jeans. A secret I can't let loose.

"Jade's a teacher," Willa tells me.

"I work with kids. Like Adare."

I stop, cheese dangling from my inky palm. It's then I know what this is all about. We've seen a lot of people like Jade. A lot of people who sit Adare at a long table, check boxes, and try to figure her out.

"Adare," Willa calls again.

Adare doesn't move and I can't decide whether I want her to stay put so they won't get a word out of her or to stand before them so we can try, one more time, to understand.

I know Mom wouldn't like Jade and her billowing skirt, someone else to tell her that Adare's wired wrong.

But Jade doesn't have a notebook or a pen. She doesn't coax Adare over and set her down. She walks over to where Adare kisses the glass.

"Hi," Adare says real fast.

"Hi, Adare." Jade levels her head to the saliva smudge. "What do you see?"

Adare has this way of pointing, like she's punishing somebody who didn't do a thing. Her finger shoots out and plucks the glass. I try to follow the line of her gaze. We all do. But with Brooklyn spread out, the river slipping wide, and the bridge stretching across, it's impossible to tell what she sees.

She dips her pointing finger into the peanut butter jar and I jump right in. "Adare, that's gross."

Willa flicks her hand at the air. "It's fine, it's fine."

I hear keys jiggle at the door. Mom's back, her shoes dropping to the floor, footsteps in the hall, until she's standing in the doorframe in her red shirt and khakis.

"Jade's here," I say before introductions can be made.

"You know Jade," Willa says to Mom, who nods and looks between them, like she knows Willa is up to something.

"Your teacher friend," Mom says.

Jade turns from the window with a little wave. "Willa's told me about you. Your family."

I wonder what she knows. About Adare being Adare. About us having no place to go.

Mom makes her way to them, ruffling my sticking-out hair. Then she wraps Adare in her arms and shakes her head. She smiles, but I watch her eyes. She's got this kind of boxing jab thing going, like she's giving them both a good scolding. "Then you know that Willa doesn't know how to leave well enough alone."

Chapter 25

In the kitchen, Mom's slamming drawers closed, then wrangling them open so the silverware rattles. Pots smack the stove and I ask if she's making *frijoles charros* again or the cookies Willa talked about—what were they?

"*Marranitos,*" she says, stern.

"You're making them?"

She whacks the lid on the pot and shakes her head. "Spaghetti."

I watch her set the jar of sauce on the counter. She leans into the cabinets, folding her arms. I can see her steaming inside, building up to a wailing teakettle, and I wonder if somehow she knows about Mrs. Belz . . . my failed test . . . remedial math.

Then she flings forward, rounds the counter into the living room, where Willa stands at the window next to Adare, pointing out the buildings, their names. Her finger rises up and traces the antenna of the Freedom Tower.

"It will never change, will it?" Mom says.

Willa looks back at her.

"Inviting Jade here." She shakes her head, disappointed. "You're always stepping in. I don't need it," she continues. "I don't need you to *save* us."

Willa looks from Mom to me, like I shouldn't be listening, but here I am. Her voice is calm. "*You* came *here.* No one forced you."

"Believe me. If there was anyone else . . ."

"Exactly," Willa says. "Where is everyone else? All your hippie *friends?*"

Mom swings her arms around the room. "Where is everyone for *you,* Willa? Where is this life that is above everyone else's? You're alone. You push everyone away."

"At least I know when I have something." She gestures at me and Adare. "To have what you have—and let it run wild . . ."

She's talking about us again. About me. I look down at my torn purple pants, ripped from climbing, and I want to say how I can't help it, how I'm just trying to get ahold of something, anything. I want to say I'm sorry for not getting it right, for sorting through numbers and not understanding how they fit into algebra. How I'm closer to being inside Daddy's tree, a place that existed when we were all together, whole. I want to say that I'm still figuring it out, but Mom says it instead.

"I'm trying," she tells Willa. "I've made mistakes, of course. But I'm trying."

Willa's quiet. "So am I."

The lid on the pot clatters. "The water's boiling," Mom announces.

But no one moves. I look at Willa and Mom and then at Adare, who isn't listening, or if she is, she doesn't seem to care. She's tucked at the foot of the window, her stomach flat against the floor, her head at the glass, peering out.

I know how it's possible to love someone you can't understand.

Mom goes to the pot and I make my way to Adare. I try to match myself up to the way she's splayed out. I notice the crows still haven't left their gifts and I ask what I never ask, the way Jade did. I whisper, "What do you see?"

She points and I follow her finger, even though I don't know where it leads. I follow it to two sets of stretching branches, their messy nests reaching out to each other, like maybe they're dancing or maybe they're tangled and caught. I say out loud what I see. "Two trees."

She breathes in, then nuzzles close to me, so close our cheeks are touching.

"Two trees," I say again. "In the dark."

Chapter 26

The next Monday, I walk down the hall slowly, letting my backpack droop from the hook of my arm. Lockers slam and the echoes have this mashed-up *wah-wah* sound to them. Like everybody's talking and no one's being heard.

I don't want to go to remedial math. I don't want to start new so late in the year. I don't want to be the one who doesn't understand.

My heels turn on the freckled floor and sunlight's trapped at the end of the hall. I stand next to my new classroom with Meredith Crane coming at me, blowing up her bangs and letting them fall to her eyebrows. She wears sparkling bracelets all up her arm. I feel my wrist for the worn plastic strap of my old watch.

Her lips slide up in a smirk. "Off to your new math class?"

"Yeah. So?"

"Everybody knows you're the most dumbest in the whole class."

"Most dumb," I say quietly.

"So you admit it."

"No—it's not *most dumbest*."

"So you *are*."

"No," I argue. "It's not grammatically correct."

I listen to her bracelets clang. "Aww." She mimics a baby voice. "Don't cry about it."

I see kids shuffling into the classroom, my new teacher at the door. I wonder why Meredith won't just let up. "I've got to go," I say, trying to move forward.

She cuts in front of me. "What's it like?" she asks. "To be a born idiot?"

"Meredith—"

"What's it like to be in the *retarded* class?"

"You should talk," I sling back.

"What are you saying?"

"I'm saying . . ." But I hesitate, not sure what I'm saying. She's got my words all mixed up.

"Are you calling *me* retarded?"

I wonder what it would matter if I said it. "Yeah. You're acting *retarded*."

Everything in Meredith goes still and I watch some kind of knowing pass in her eyes. She stands on her tiptoes and twirls around to my new classroom.

"*Ms. Viti-eeellooo!*" she calls, shrieky and high, like a song out of tune. "She called me a bad name!"

Ms. Vitiello peers from the door, with big, wide bangs and square glasses. She's dressed in tight jet-black, looking more like a lady in a comic than a teacher. "What's this about?" She has an accent like the voices on the Beatles songs Mom listens to.

My face gets hot and the word sits, splattered, at my feet. I try and find something to say, but my voice is gone.

"She called me . . ." Then she whispers it, like a secret. ". . . *retarded*. She said it, clear as day."

"She started it," I say.

Ms. Vitiello looks at each of us and then settles on me. My face blazes red-hot candy. "We don't use language like that here."

"She should get marked up," Meredith chimes in.

"She should get to class." Then she juts her chin out at Meredith. "As a matter of fact, you both should."

Meredith smirks at me and runs off. I stand rooted.

"Are you coming or going?" Ms. Vitiello asks me.

I don't move. How can I walk in there now?

"You need to get to your next class."

I realize she doesn't know I'm meant to be here with her.

"Consider this a warning."

I nod and run toward the stairwell, pushing the metal-barred door.

Chapter 27

I sit on the stairs, tucked in a corner. Sun from a small crack of window lights the stairwell an old blue. Strands of dust curl around like mice tails. I clutch my Tree Book and listen for anyone prowling around, thinking up excuses. *I'm coming from the nurse's office. . . . I was late this morning. . . . They called me down to the principal's office.* I fold a piece of paper and keep it caught between my fingers, like I'm holding a hall pass.

My body goes cold, thinking about what I said, how it could just be a word. *Special* like *species. Retarded* like *slow.* But I know it's not just a word. It's a way of labeling somebody *different.* It's a way of labeling somebody *wrong.*

I'm all confused, thinking how sometimes Adare *is* different. Sometimes Adare *is* wrong, holding her pencil up over her homework page and not writing a thing down.

But I can't get at the right answers, either. Not in math, not up in the tree, not from Mom, not from anybody.

I open my palm and let my fake hall pass fall. I take my pen and draw the mess of me. A knot. Like the busted-up rope along the canal.

Footsteps start knocking and I shoot up from sitting, smearing my pen-inked palm. I glance upstairs and downstairs, wondering which way is best and what I'll say when I get to where I'm going and where I'll go next before the bell rings again and I can get back to where I belong.

The feet come closer, slide past me, and then stop. I see Sabina's braids flip as she turns to face me. She's got a proper hall pass. A wooden block with a string. "I was wondering where you were."

"What are you doing here?" I ask before she can ask more about me.

"Bathroom."

"Can't you use the third-floor bathroom?"

"Sure. But this way takes longer. Why aren't you in Mrs. Belz's class?"

I realize she doesn't know where I'm supposed to be, so I shrug. "Just didn't go."

"You *cut*?"

Cut. "I didn't mean to," I say quietly. "It just happened."

I expect her to laugh, to move on, to accept things the

way they are, like when I told her we didn't really have a place to live and she didn't even care. But she's looking like she can't believe anyone would do something like that, waiting for some kind of explanation I don't know how to give. She shakes her head. "Cora."

And that's all she says. Just my name. It's like a scolding, hearing it like that. Hearing who I am. The kind of kid who fails tests and cuts classes. Who doesn't belong at Sabina's kitchen table doing homework.

"You wouldn't understand," I say. "You've got a reading hour and a homework timer and everything. . . ." My voice trails away and I don't know how else to explain.

We stay like this, all silent, and I feel the weight of my name, the way she said it, all disappointed.

I know that one small thing can become one big thing. Like not knowing *a*, and soon you've landed in remedial math. Like not listening to your little sister in a cupcake shop, and then you're watching her hold her breath. Like a heart growing just a little too big, and then a person's gone.

I think of that note we found—Jess and Becca. This could be the start of things falling apart.

I stand up fast, not wanting to know. "You'd better go," I say.

She nods. "Yeah. Maybe I'll see you later?" She asks like she's not sure.

I don't know the answer, either. "Maybe?" I ask back.

"Sure."

But it feels a whole lot different from that first time she told me she'd see me on Monday, like it was obvious, of course. She turns around, the squeak of her rubber soles echoing in the stairwell while I wait for the bell to ring, with a mangled knot in my palm.

Chapter 28

After school, I'm quick to pick up Adare so we can get to the tree of heaven. Maybe Willa thinks we're running wild, but I'm only trying to figure out how things stay put. Adare nudges her fingers through mine again, the opposite of how I like it. It makes it harder to guide her and I feel like we're all twisted. But I walk fast, wanting to forget the day, the way Sabina looked at me, and the wrong words getting loose. I want to get back to the tree.

We pass Miss Li's and walk along the bent fence, below the subway tracks, over the bridge, and back to the narrow path along the canal.

I kneel down at the fallen tree. Sabina's collection of notes sits in neat squares and I pick one from the top of a stack. It's a phone number on frilly, flowered paper. The handwriting is so neat, it looks like a typewritten memo. I wonder if it was lost before or after the call.

I place it back. The screech owl's gone, but the charcoal cat's here, stretched out in a line of sun, his legs all pointing in one direction, on his side, almost like he's dead, but his tail flips back and forth, so we know he's not. Adare sits beside him. Before I can stop her, she's chucking her shoes off. One pink high-top lands on the other, and she's spreading her clean white socks in the dirt. I wonder how I'll explain this one.

I make my way to the wobbling dock. I have to get into the tree. I balance my walk on the dock and snatch at the busted-up rope there, trying to untie its hard, worn knot from the post.

But I can't untie it. It's stuck together with the glue of years and rain and the oil sludge of the canal.

"It won't budge!" I tell Adare—because who else am I going to tell but Adare?—who is now flat on her back, red hair woven in strands of dirt. She strokes the cat's belly with her hand.

"You're making a mess of yourself."

She laughs and arches her back, so she can see farther into the deep, cloudy sky.

"You're pretty useless, you know."

As soon as I say it, I regret it, but I don't know what makes me angrier—that I keep words like that in my heart or that Adare stays smiling and doesn't seem to care.

I kick at the dirt, hoping to dig up something. Anything. Adare's sleeping anger. A rope. A ladder.

But there's just wet newspaper, a swirl of dirt, colored plastic, and a ratty pair of red sunglasses, muddy and split.

I stomp over and stand at the tree, looking up at the first notch my foot can get to. It's just too high. I place my hand on the tree's rough skin. Then I toe my rubber sneakers at the base. But the trunk's too wide and there's nothing to grip.

Across the canal the houseboats sit in a line, in their paper-lantern string, and I know that Sabina and Jacob are somewhere in there. It'll be snack time or homework time and they'll be sitting with their notes and their timer, doing the right thing, while I'm running wild out here, just like Willa said.

I walk the patches of wild grass to the edge of the red warehouse. Behind it the junkyard sits like forgotten homework.

I pace back, then sit beside Adare.

I need to think about getting into the tree a different way. Like Sabina standing on her head. An *inversion*. I need to think with my head below my heart and my feet at the sky.

I flip onto my hands, fingernails clutching at the dirt. Blood's rushing to my head, and my feet waver. My arms start to shake. I try to swallow and it's like gravity thinks I'm nuts.

Adare laughs and I scold her. "It's not funny. There's no way up."

"Yeah," she says, as if there *is* a way. She points and I follow her arm, arching my neck, to the old red warehouse.

The roof.

"The roof," I say out loud. I slip back to my feet and look to Adare, her smile almost as big as mine is becoming.

The inverse.

If I can't climb up, I'll just have to get to the roof and climb down.

Chapter 29

"I've got to get to the roof," I tell Adare, who nods fast, like she cares more about this than I thought, like maybe we're in this together.

"Yeah," she says.

The red warehouse looks kind of like a barn or a big old shed where people keep things they don't use. I circle the edges. The grass rides up and tickles my knees.

"We need to find a door," I say. But there's only lumber leaning up against the shingles.

I can see the junkyard and the excavators with their bending yellow arms, elbows pointing up. There's nobody around, but it feels like somebody was just here, everything left in midair, like a frozen television screen.

There's a huge, loud rumbling sound as I turn another corner and there's a door propped open a little. I know we need to get in, no matter what, because I need to be in that tree. I need to understand the magic of what's inside.

I knock, but the door is thick and strange and my knuckles make barely any sound. So I take a deep breath and push the door open wide, into the cold, heavy brick room.

A gigantic pink structure touches the ceiling, which is so high, I get dizzy looking up into the rafters.

There are people in big rubber boots and silver space suits, their clear helmets snapped shut over their faces. They hold long wood poles with barrels attached to them and I don't know whether to stay or go. There are shouts and echoes and it's warm, and as I look up at the giant pink stone, I watch men in their boots and gloves dangling from a pair of ladders like acrobats.

The rumbling sound gets inside my chest and I feel the heat before I see it. The barrels burn orange and spill fire, like they're pouring angry sunlight. Sparks fly and flicker and fall to the ground and I let out a yelp without meaning to, thinking I should run, but something in me, some kind of knowing and wishing, stands firm.

There's a shout. "Hey!"

Then "Hold up!"

And they turn their giant rods. The fire settles back upright into its burning cauldron. The low rumbling quiets.

A woman in boots and gloves pulls the helmet from

her face. Her hair is in spooling ropes, piled on top of her head. "What's this?"

Then I realize she's pointing at us, we're the *this*. I stand, frozen in the doorway.

"Get out or come on in!" she yells.

So I do what I know best. I grab Adare's hand and run as fast as I can.

As I do, I feel the blanketed sky break apart, the clouds wringing out rain. The raindrops are at my cheeks, running like tears to the dirt and the roots and all the things just trying their best to inch up.

I hear Adare let out an excited shriek. She's all laughter and rain as the cat slinks toward the fallen tree for shelter. I see Sabina's note stacks, all safe and dry.

Adare spreads her arms out, spinning around an imaginary maypole. She dances a Brooklyn rain dance next to the red warehouse. I stare at her and wonder what gets inside her like that, what makes her feel like, wherever she is, she belongs.

Chapter 30

"The tree's our secret, right?" I ask Adare after we rush to the subway steps and squeak through the turnstile, shaking our wet coats and hair over the platform, dripping a puddle on the train floor. "And the fire."

I help her put her shoes back on, and she looks at me with a wide grin, her hair in a frizz. Then she nods, like she's just decided. "Okay."

"When people find something rare in nature, they don't tell anybody the exact spot," I explain, more to myself than anyone. "That's so no one'll go and ruin it."

"Yeah."

"And the cat," I remind her. "That's our secret, too."

She nods. "I love him."

"Whatever you say, Adare."

She seems satisfied with that, so I feel satisfied, too.

Maybe Adare and I don't need our crows if we have this secret to share.

When we leave the subway, the rain has stopped and the sky is a mushy, soft gray, like it's getting ready to turn dark. I scan trees. There are ginkgoes, Norway maples, and Callery pears.

Then I push through the revolving doors and smile at the doorman. My shoes are slippery. The rubber squawks the way Sabina's boots do and we slip into the elevator, press the button, and rise up, passing floors.

When we twist the key to Willa's apartment, Adare starts giggling and rips her shoes off, throwing her sopping wet socks in the air, tossing her coat in a heap on the floor. I try to straighten her pink high-tops in the line of shoes Willa keeps in the entrance. I place her jacket on the hook just as I see her clothes in a hopscotch pattern on the hall floor, polka-dot leggings, a hoodie, and a T-shirt. Adare's running in her underwear through the apartment, laughing.

Mom peeks her head around the wall. "What's going on here?"

Adare wraps her arms around her bare chest and leans in with a whisper. "Rain."

"I see that." Then she looks to me for an explanation.

"Just climbing again," I tell her. "We got caught in the rain."

"You know I don't like you climbing in the rain. You could slip."

She leans against the white wall, holding a steaming cup of tea in her hands. Adare stands in her underwear, her hair leaping every which way.

"How about a nice bath?" Mom asks.

Adare crinkles her forehead. She's too used to standing in curtainless shower stalls where the hot water only works half the time.

"Let's try it," she says, and Adare shrugs, then slides down on her naked tummy across the hardwood floor, looking for Sookie.

While Mom runs the bath, I sit on the shining white tiles with my Tree Book. My scribbles are silly symbols and a sloppy script of words. There are lines of crooked branches and bent flowers, a daffodil with a miniature bell in the center, because that's how it looks. All of it means something, but only to me. And Daddy's numbers and calculations tell the story of a garden that doesn't grow anymore.

Willa's tub has four silver feet that look like a cat's paws. It seems like something from an antique shop, but it gleams as if it's had a makeover.

When the tub is full, Mom slaps her knees and stands up. Then she holds out a piece of paper, folded in a neat little square. I recognize it right away. The note from Mrs. Belz.

"I found it doing laundry," she says. "When were you going to tell me?"

I shake my head. "I'm sorry."

"If you need help, you come to me, Cora."

"When? When's the right time to talk about math when you've got too many other things to worry about?"

"This is as important as anything. *More* important, even."

"Me being smart, you mean? Me getting it right?"

"No, Cora. You understanding. You staying on track. It's important, given our circumstances." Then she sighs. "I dropped out of school," she tells me. "Willa hated me for it. *I* hate me for it. Don't make that mistake."

I nod. *On track.* Not off it. Not like the kind of kid who cuts her first class of remedial math.

"When do you start the class?" she asks.

I hesitate. I don't mention today. I can't. I say, "The day after tomorrow. We've got an assembly."

She looks at me, squinting, like she's trying to figure me out. "I want to hear all about it." Then she pulls out the other piece of paper, my crumpled test of fingernail moons. "Your drawings are beautiful, Cora."

I snatch it from her, feeling embarrassed by the answerless test.

She points to my book. "You haven't run out of pages yet?"

I shake my head. "Not yet." But I look warily at what's left. Even the margins of old pages are filling up with my scribbles.

"He was very meticulous, your father."

I start writing what I know so far. *Tree of heaven. No buds. Mid-March.*

"He wanted to understand all the living things he studied. The land, for him, was a science. It's not like that for us, is it?"

I pause, my pencil caught in a loop of script.

"We go by how we feel, in here." I watch her place her hand on her heart. "And Willa's place, it feels . . ."

"Right." I finish her sentence at the same time that she says, "Wrong."

She calls for Adare. Then we sit with the quiet.

"I love Willa. But she's . . ." Mom searches for words. "Judgy. She judges, not just for herself. For others, too."

I think of her giving me money for the MetroCard and having Jade visit.

"She thinks she knows best. She thinks I don't know what I'm doing with my life."

"Do you?" I ask.

"It's not easy, Cora. Doing this on my own. But things are steady at the store. I'm on track to a promotion. To manager. Working with displays. We're going to find a safe place, somewhere, that's ours. Not Willa's."

"But it's easy here," I say, trying to convince her anyway.

"*Easy* isn't what we're made of," she says.

I wonder why what we're made of has to be so hard. I think there's got to be a part of me that fits in easy right here.

"I don't remember his voice," I say.

Mom is quiet.

"And his face is a blur." I hold out my Tree Book. "But he left us what he knew and I've mapped out everywhere we've ever been." I flip through the pages. "I know everything that grows here." I swallow hard. I say what I have to say. "We need time," I tell her. "In one place. We need seasons. That's the only way to make it work. We need to stay."

"Maybe you're right."

"I am."

Mom reaches out for my hand. "What do we have today?"

I hold open my palm. My blurry knot.

"What is it?"

I look at the misshapen blob and think of all the *wrong* of today. Cutting class, getting off track, spouting words I never meant to say.

Adare bounds in and leans over the tub, smacking her hands against the pool of water.

"I don't know," I say, even though I know it's just the mess inside of me.

"It's something," Mom tells me. "Keep going."

Chapter 31

The next day, I make my way back to the canal with Adare.

It's drizzling this misting kind of spray, and it leaves a sheen on our cheeks and frizzes up my hair. Adare does her usual stop-and-go toward the canal, like a Coney Island bumper car, and I sigh at every stop.

The mist reminds me of the way I used to spray the leaves in my greenhouse and I tell Adare, "I've got to get in the warehouse. I think it's the only way up."

"Okay." Then her bright, shining eyes darken. We both look toward the houseboats and I wonder why I didn't see Sabina at lunch, why she barely even waved when I passed her in the hall on my way to art.

Adare and I circle the warehouse together and approach the door. This time, when I push it open, no one is standing around in a space suit. It's quiet and the barrels aren't lit. They hang in the gray of the room, with its dim light and cold stone floor. There are tables with wood and metal and paper thrown across them. The giant pink sculpture still races to the ceiling, but now it's in the shape of a skinny, narrow, misshapen heart.

A woman sits, her hair in big, wound dreadlocks. She's the woman who yelled out yesterday. She sits hunched over the messy table in the corner.

I leave the doorway and walk toward her, Adare still holding tight to my hand. I don't know whether to let my voice boom out in the echoing room or what. I'm saved the trouble when Adare calls out her famous "Hi."

The woman squints through the room. "Can I help you?"

Yes, I think, and then I let myself say it. "Yes. I need to get to the roof."

She looks us over. My tangled hair and a sunflower backpack strapped to my shoulders. Adare with her big mirror eyes. The woman folds her arms. "What for?"

"I've got to get in a tree," I tell her.

I look up to where Adare keeps staring. At the ceiling. At the top of the giant metal heart. The right side of the heart is angled and edged, crooked and strange, but the left side is smoothed into a perfect arch.

"Sounds important." She unfolds her arms. Then she

follows my gaze to the heart and points. "What do you think of it?"

"It's tall." I tell her what I see. "The two sides don't match."

"That's right. They don't."

"Shouldn't they?"

"More often they don't."

I can't help but think of Daddy, how even the biggest of hearts can fail you in the worst way. "You made it like this on purpose?" I ask.

She nods. "I had help. This place is a foundry. For shaping metal. You saw everyone here, shaping it into what I need it to be."

"So that's what everyone was doing in space suits?"

She laughs. "Space suits . . . I guess so."

"Is it art?" I ask.

"I don't know. What do you think?"

I tilt my head at the towering heart, with its two sides that don't match. Mom says art is something made. Something that makes you think or feel a little spark of wonder inside. "I think it is." Then I ask, "Is it *your* heart?"

She tilts her head and smiles. "You could say that, yes. A little crooked. A little confused. But big. Or at least trying to be. You know?" She asks it like she really cares to hear the answer, so I think about the unfinished drawing in my palm, my trying as best I can, and I tell her, "Yup.

I understand. My mom was an artist. She painted murals around here. Liana Quinn. Have you heard of her?"

She shakes her head. "No."

"Oh."

She takes her hands to her hips. "So what is this about needing to get in a tree?"

"It was my dad's tree, once. The tree of heaven. He studied it right up until he died."

She looks like she's thinking. Then I remember she's an artist, so I try a new way of explaining. I reach into my bag and dig for my Tree Book. I hold it out. "I'm a climber," I explain, and I say it the way Mom did that night in Willa's kitchen, like I'm proud.

"Tough break, being a climber along the Gowanus Canal. Not much grows here. And a lot of trees got lost in the storm a few years back."

"But this one's still here."

"Then it must be strong." She stands up. She wears a lot of scarves wrapped around her shoulders and hanging in fringe from her neck. Her heavy boots knock the floor.

"Well, I'm afraid I can't help. I don't own the place. I'm renting it until we have our exhibition. That's all."

"Oh." I feel my negotiation hitting a dead end.

She reaches her hand out to me for a shake. "I'm Anju."

But it's Adare who takes her hand and, instead of

shaking it, runs her fingers across the sparkling gold rings and funky round stones.

"This is Adare," I say for her.

Anju doesn't snatch her hand away. She takes her other hand and closes it around Adare's instead. "And you are?" she asks me.

"Cora."

She smiles. *"El corazón."*

This is one of the Spanish words I know, so I say it out loud. "Heart."

"And the name of my piece."

I look up into the rafters, to her heart, the top of her *piece.* There are pipes running all along the ceiling and sprinkler knobs in case of fire. I see a ladder attached to the wall that snakes up high and I see it lead to the vaulted roof.

I'm about to open my mouth and point out the ladder. But maybe it's better as a secret. Maybe Anju doesn't want a climber in her rented space. Maybe I'll have to get there when she's gone.

"Wait a minute—did you say Liana?" she asks.

I nod. "Yeah, why?"

"There was a mural artist who painted all along the walls of community gardens. Liana Reyes."

My eyes grow wide. Mom's name before she was married. "That's my mom."

"So you're an artist, like her?"

I nod and blush. "I guess."

"Cool. Well, I hope you get in that tree," she tells me. "I really do."

I smile, thinking that now I've found the ladder, I will.

Chapter 32

"There's roof access. For sure."

Adare nods, which gets me even more excited, thinking I'm getting closer to where I'm supposed to be.

Then she rips her hand from mine and sends it soaring, following a line of flapping black as it disappears. "Crows," she says quietly.

"Yours?" I wonder out loud.

But her gaze has already dropped. She runs outside the lines of the canal like some kind of taking-off crayon.

"Adare, you come back here!" I've got no choice but to follow as she takes the narrow path and crosses the Ninth Street Bridge, curling around to the other side of the canal where Sabina's houseboat sits in the oozing water.

She stands in front of the boat, lingers for a second. I call out from behind, "Adare, stop right there! We're not invited."

But she runs from the dock onto the boat, slips through the little door, and slams it.

I walk to the door and knock, then realize, with Adare already in there, that doesn't make any sense, so I let myself in, feeling my cheeks go red and hot. I dip my head and everyone stares up at the two of us.

Sabina and Jacob sit on the floor with their homework. Mrs. Griffin sits in a hard-backed chair with some kind of knitting.

"I'm sorry—I don't—" But I don't know what to say, don't know why we're here, so I just grab at Adare's wrist. She shakes her head and stomps her foot and the boat wavers slightly. She points at those stupid chimes again, not knowing the word, or knowing it but not wanting to say.

Mrs. Griffin smiles. "Cora. Adare. It's so good of you to stop by."

There's the vague smell of fish. The boat is murky and damp. I hadn't noticed that before.

"I didn't know you were coming," Sabina says, and I can't tell whether she's happy I'm here or not.

I look from Adare, all wild and dirty and stomping and whining, to Sabina, in her pretty puff skirt and boots, quietly doing her schoolwork. "No, we've got to go. Adare is just . . ." I'm not sure how to explain.

"We've got graham crackers." Mrs. Griffin motions toward the pantry. "Cinnamon."

"No, it's okay. We need to go."

But Adare will not move. She's staring at the chimes. Something about them has caught her attention—their sparkle, their sound. I don't know, have never known, what it means to live inside Adare's mind.

"I think it's your chimes," I tell them, my face getting more and more red. "She wants to see them, hear them—I don't know."

I move toward the chimes and let my fingers slip through the glass. The sound shimmers. As they ring, Adare runs her own fingers through them. She circles them as the glass catches the small hints of sun.

The sound ripples again. Even Mrs. Griffin looks on in wonder and surprise. She talks to Adare gently, like a teacher. "The chimes sound when the water's choppy," she tells her. "When it storms."

I try to imagine this boat in a storm. The swell and flicker of never-ending chimes. I remember Daddy talking about rainfall, not the good kind the earth needs but the bad kind, the kind that can ruin everything.

"Is that all you wanted?" I ask Adare. "To hear them?"

"The crows," she says like everyone will understand.

"Who?" Mrs. Griffin asks.

"The crows," she repeats.

"Oh, crows." Mrs. Griffin encourages her. "Yes. They do like shiny things."

I think of all the trinkets the crows left Adare, all of them silver and shining, and I realize as the chimes shimmer and ripple, dancing their light across the walls, I need to do a better job of trying to understand.

I reach my hand out to Adare and say to the Griffins, "I'm sorry." Then I shrug, like it can't be helped, because nothing about us can. "We didn't mean to barge in."

Before they can say anything more, before Sabina can try to even catch my eye, I look down, fast, and Adare and I dip our heads to fit through the little door.

Chapter 33

The next day, I walk to remedial math with my washed-away *a* from all those days ago, with all the missing letters that should be numbers. I take a deep breath as I round a corner in the halls, preparing to let Ms. Vitiello know that when she asked the other morning, I should have been going one way: to her class.

As I'm running over it in my head, I hear the shimmer of dangling bracelets. I don't know what I did to deserve it, but I swear I'm walking straight at Meredith Crane again. The girl is blowing up her bangs like a steam engine.

"Yes," I sigh, and say, before she can, "I'm off to remedial. Don't go on about it."

"Long as Ms. Vitiello knows what a name-calling fool you are."

I shake my head and keep walking until something in me can't let it go. "You know, Meredith, sometimes you've got to work at a thing. It doesn't come natural. For example, math," I say.

"Okay, like, what are you, some kind of philosopher?"

I keep going. "Or being nice. Sometimes you have to work at that. If I were you, I'd start trying."

She looks like she's about to shoot her mouth off again, but then I watch her clamp it shut. She slides her bracelets up and down her arm, adjusts her backpack, and turns away.

I walk to class, planning what I'll say to Ms. Vitiello about Meredith Crane getting the best of me the other day when she shouldn't have, about needing to get on track because of my *circumstances*. But when I walk in, she's got a smile so soft, it could be Adare's, and she talks before I do.

"Cora Quinn," she states, and I nod. "This where you're supposed to be?"

I look around at all the kids, one clacking a pencil like a drumstick against the metal desk, another looking so far out the window, it's like she's not even here. A little bit like Adare. A little bit like me. "Yes," I say. "And I'm sorry, Ms. Vitiello. The other day—"

She waves her hand. She makes it seem like she knows already, like she even knew that day. "You can call me Ms. Alice." She surveys me through the space above the dip of her glasses. "I do things a little differently than Mrs. Belz," she tells me. "I have different rules."

Rules. I don't like the sound of that.

"The first is that I don't ask the questions in this room. *You* do."

I'm quiet, despite feeling confused. But I nod fast.

"You'll see how it works." Then the bell rings and everyone shuffles in and I try not to think about how I miss Sabina's wailing boots or even Meredith Crane's clanking eraser. I pull out my Tree Book and quickly survey the new view from here.

It's the first day of spring.

"Shall we begin?" She looks to us for approval and *Yes*es murmur their way across the room.

Her chalk on the board is easy and looping as she writes out equations.

I make sure to pay attention. I make sure not to look off and away.

Her hand swirls across the board, creating a small, simple, numberless equation: $a + b = c$.

Then she turns, places her hand on her hip, and looks at us. The quiet has this kind of wonder in it as she scans the room. "Someone ask the first question."

No one budges.

"I'll give you a hint. It's easiest to start from the end. Start backward."

The girl who was staring out the window throws her hand up in the air. "What's c?"

Ms. Alice erases c and makes it a 6. Then she boomerangs her chalk back, pointing at us.

"What's b?" someone calls out.

Ms. Alice erases the b and makes it a 4.

What's a? My heart thumps, but I don't call out and Ms. Alice has already moved on. "We have our first facts," she tells us. "$a = 2$ and $b = 4$."

She writes this down, setting it up in the corner with a squiggle cloud around each, like we've solved the first piece of a puzzle. "Keep track," she tells us. "In your notes. Of the facts."

And we play this way for the rest of the class, everyone calling out questions while Ms. Alice gives us answers, assigning numbers to letters. I watch chalk markings disappear with the quick swipe of her eraser. I watch every letter become a number. I watch the facts fill up on the side of the board in their squiggle clouds. It feels like a game, throwing out questions, erasing letters, assigning numbers, and gaining a fact.

Then Ms. Alice writes a long equation across the board, an impossible string of letters and numbers, longer than any equation Mrs. Belz ever gave us.

She turns to us, hand-hipped, her smile pink and easy. "Now," she says. "I need each of you to find a. Write it down with your name on a slip of paper and hand it to me when the bell rings."

I stare back in disbelief.

"You have all the facts. You gave them to me."

I scan the running, messy string. I keep an eye on the squiggle clouds.

"There are no secrets in algebra. There are no tricks. Just puzzles. Just tricky ways of arranging. Everything you need is right there."

I stare at the equation. Letters and numbers. Parentheses. Squares. I realize that for every empty letter, there's a way of filling it up if I start with Ms. Alice's first hint. *Start backward.*

When it clicks, it clicks, Mom said. And the answer comes, quick and fast, my pencil scrawling across the lined paper, threatening to fly off onto the desk because there isn't enough room—there's never enough room—for the long, rattling takeoff of a thing growing. And when I reach a kind of end, which is really a beginning, I know exactly what *a* is.

Before I place the number 7 on a small square of paper, I draw it in my palm first. I stare at it, the number 7, with its leaning straight stalk and its flying leaf. I close it and keep it. *Found.*

Chapter 34

After mucking in the dirt and drizzling rain while climbing street trees, I hold on to Adare with one hand and the 7 in my other palm. I can't wait to explain to Mom how it's a number for a letter I never thought I'd find, how I sent myself backward to work ahead. I want to tell her about the tree of heaven, about Anju, how she's an artist just like Mom is. Like maybe I am, too.

When the elevator doors slide open, I don't have to scan the little gold letters anymore to Willa's. I know how we turn the corners and pass the sparkling mirrors that guide us straight toward it. I know how 12B has a pair of tall rain boots slumped over by the door. I wait for the waft of Willa's coconut soap, which has this way of slipping through the air to the hallway.

But when we get there, the smell is muffled and the door's wide open and I see a bag propping it up.

We walk in and Willa stands with arms crossed. "Does it have to be such a whirlwind?"

"This is how we live, Willa." Mom smiles at us and I watch her zip up an old knapsack. My stomach flutters with knowing and I wonder if I should even take my backpack off.

Adare runs dirt across the floor toward Mom and wraps her arms around her waist in a big hug. I stand at the door, watching our things evolve into neat piles.

"Tilda's found us a new placement in Red Hook," she tells me.

Placement. I hate the word. Like we're a rubber band in a junk drawer, being shoved into someplace no one else wants to be.

Everything in me tightens and I feel like I can't move, like I have to stand beside the doorframe, between the hallway and Willa's, because if I step forward or backward, I'll scream. So I just start with a slow shake of my head, the whisper of my *No* battering down the door to my chest, trying to escape.

"You can stay here," Willa tells her.

"We can't."

"At least think about Jade's school. Jade says she can pull a few strings, get Adare in. It's a good school, Liana. She'll do it as a favor. For me."

"I'll think about it," she says. "Of course."

Adare's butterfly wings are folded in half. They sit on

the plumped-up quilt. I have the urge to rip them apart, to spread the quilt out and crumple myself beneath it, with the fabric at my ears the way we puff up Adare's sheets, inside a place that's dark and small and safe and mine.

I wonder why Willa couldn't keep her nose out of our business, quit worrying about special schools and Metro-Cards.

As Mom unravels from Adare's embrace, she sees the tracks of mud. She sees Adare's ankles, gray dirt caked at the fold of her socks, and her leggings soaked straight through. "You're a filthy mess," she tells her, and Adare starts giggling. Then she looks to me. "You both are."

I say nothing. I stay tight-lipped, the way Adare does when she doesn't feel like answering or doing her homework or explaining herself out of the old patches of dirt we get ourselves in.

"You know I don't like you climbing in the rain."

I close my eyes and wait behind their shuttered walls. I want a snack from the refrigerator. I want to press my nose against the cold glass and stare out at the tugboats, down into the tops of the trees. I imagine myself falling through the glass and down onto the canopy, nesting myself in strands of soft leaves.

I hear Mom's feet scamper toward the kitchen, hear the roll of paper towels as she rips a few sheets off. "We should get cleaned up before we leave. I don't know what—" But she stops herself and I listen to all she doesn't say. She doesn't know what we'll find when we get to where nobody else wants to be. She doesn't know what will be ours. She doesn't know anything.

"I'll give Adare a bath. Wash your hands. Get together your clothes. In a pile. *Neat*," she scolds before she needs to.

Adare giggles.

I don't move.

"Come on, Cora. I'd like to get going."

I don't open my eyes. I don't say all I want to say. *No. No. I want to stay here.*

Instead, I ask what I really want to know, with my eyes still closed and my voice quiet. "Why are you making us leave?"

"This place is Willa's," she tells me. "Not ours."

I listen as Adare's laughter plows down the hallway toward the bathroom, then open my eyes to the room and our batches of things.

Mom follows Adare, and I squat to the floor, take my filthy hands and shovel my clothes into my backpack while Willa looks on. I don't want to let her eyes meet mine.

"You okay?" Willa asks.

I don't answer.

"You can visit, you know. Anytime you want."

I pull at the zipper, but it's broken and won't budge.

"I was the first in my family to go to college. Heck, your mother and I were the first in our families to leave the *state*."

I don't know why it matters, why she's telling me this. I'm tugging at the zipper, trying to yank it closed.

"What I'm saying is, you have to go beyond your experience to find out what you need and where you belong. And then, even when you do, you're still figuring it out."

I push my bunched-up clothes to the bottom of the backpack and try to cinch it closed with my fist.

"Your mother and I, we're more alike than you might think. We're people who go looking."

I smack the bag down and watch the clothes spill over as Willa takes my shoulders. She shifts me around, looks me in the eyes. "There's no *one* place, Cora. Remember that."

When she lets go, I say, "There has to be."

She takes my hand in hers. "Don't worry," she tells me. "Someday you'll see."

Chapter 35

Our *placement,* Mom says, is not a shelter. It's real housing for people like us who don't have much but are trying to work steady. It's west of the canal in Red Hook. I can tell because we ride along the river, looking out with Manhattan on our right. This place pushes out toward the harbor, at the hook of Brooklyn, and we have to take the B61 bus.

I haven't said a word since we walked out of Willa's, our entire world shoved into bags, like always, slung over our shoulders, dragged from one sad place to the next. When we leave, I feel like a slotted spoon, losing all its drippings, left with only thick, gross chunks. Willa said goodbye and told us she couldn't *wait* to come visit. She and Mom hugged as Mom whispered a thank-you and her hand slipped from her heart.

I know this is the way we do things. I know this is how

we leave our mark. We leave places empty. We leave them so it's like we've never been anywhere.

We sit on the blue seats of the bus and pass the old warehouses on the docks, the metal fences, the overgrown grass, still brown and left over from last winter. There are buildings with the windows gone and there's a cruise ship with its nose nudging the edge of the harbor and there aren't so many trees, just the gray horizon at the slapping water, holding on to the sun before it sets.

"You'll stay in school," Mom tells me, "at least until the end of the year. So you don't have to worry about that."

I hadn't worried. I hadn't let myself. I assumed I'd be sent somewhere new—and what would it matter? I don't have anyone here.

I stay quiet. I practice at being Adare.

I try not to let myself think of Willa, but I do. I let myself remember how she wanted us and held on to a piece of who Mom used to be. Now we've left it behind. What happens to that piece?

I fold my arms tighter at my chest and feel the dirt under my fingernails. My hair is still tangled wet with rain. I refused to shower, even though it may have been my last chance. And it's that thought, of all things, that makes my eyes sting, but I press my arms closer to my chest, like I'm holding on to my insides, begging them to stay put.

I hate that the bus makes loud, squealing sounds as we round corners. I hate that we have to pull the black cord if we want it to stop. I like the subway to Willa's better.

When we get to our stop, Mom reaches for both our hands, but Adare's clutching Sookie and I pull mine away. I wish I'd smudged the 7 on my palm because I don't want to share it. I shift my bag from one hand to the other, wrapping my 7 around it.

I don't look at trees. I don't want to place us here.

Mom looks up to the sky. "Good. We'll get there before dark."

She holds tight to Adare and I hold tight to a bag of things that don't even feel like my own.

We make our way to a crown of buildings that don't look any different from Ennis House. There might not be an Old Lou, but in the crisscross paths of the courtyard there are people with lost stares, leaning on the empty bicycle racks and against the building.

The doors are heavy, and like Ennis House, the halls are dim. The walls peel their layers of blue and gray paint. The steel railings of the staircase are spattered brown. As I prepare to climb the steps, Mom points at a narrow tan door. "Come on—we'll take the elevator."

It's not like Willa's. We open the door like it's a cubby, and we step into the filthy box, which smells like urine and old sweat. When Mom presses 3, a set of brass-looking bars scratch closed and it sounds like a broken machine trying to do something that doesn't need to be done. At the third floor, the bars slide back and disappear, and we push open the door and step into the hall.

It doesn't smell like Fred C.'s McDonald's or like the new carpet of Willa's. It smells like soup sitting on top of the stove and chicken frying and spices all mangled up. It smells like *now,* like tonight. Like tomorrow will be different, depending on dinner.

Mom scans the hall, looking from one closed door to the next.

The apartments are closer together than they are at Willa's but not as close as at Ennis House.

It's the last apartment, in a corner, next to a window shielded by metal bars. The number of the apartment is faded and scratched, like it's not a real address at all.

Mom pulls a silver key from the breast pocket of her coat.

"Can we have our own?" I whisper.

"Maybe. We'll see."

Then she opens the door to our *placement,* which is as gray and sad as any other place we've been. There's a stove, which is better than a hot plate, and a bathroom, but when I peek in, there's no inner tube for our toothbrushes.

I make my way to the window, looking for something, anything, that will make this place feel like ours. But there's just the slim crevice between our building and the next slab of brick. A row of pigeons purr so loud, it's like a chorus of sad sighs.

I don't look at Mom to see how she sees this place. I decide for myself. This is not where I want to be.

Chapter 36

I wake up beneath our quilt, on an air mattress Mom got discounted from the store. Someone returned it with a hole and she patched it with Band-Aids—the kiddie kind, with flowers and Snoopy and Mickey Mouse.

Some morning light steals in from between the two sets of buildings. A line of yellow extends across the hardwood floor, splitting Adare's soft, sleeping face in half.

I won't be able to grow anything with only one narrow slice of sun. Still, I sit up, quiet, and reach for my backpack. I smooth the pages of my Tree Book and draw the skinny line.

It's only then that I realize Mom's awake, standing at the window with her steaming purple mug of tea. I remember it's March twenty-first, the day after the first day of spring, which makes her sad because it's the day Daddy *left this world,* as she says, and I know that on some days you can feel a person *gone* more than on others. Some days you can only feel someone in your heart, when all you want to do is hold that person's hand.

She makes her way over and I shut the book closed, crushing it to my chest, not wanting her to see any part of what's mine.

"I never asked what we had," she says, nudging her finger to my palm.

I open it in the dim light and hold it out to her. My number 7. It's faded, so it looks like a smudge of disappearing ink. I don't feel proud of it anymore. What does it matter if I found the answer to something I should have found months ago?

She holds my hand in hers and her smile is sad. "You'll see," she whispers. "Tomorrow I'll have this place done up right. I know it's not like Willa's. But it's not like the shelters, either. It's more like ours."

I wonder what will make this place feel like ours. Everything we've ever owned was someone else's before.

"I know it's not perfect," she says. "But I see what it can be. Can't you?"

I shake my head, letting my palm fall from hers. "No."

Chapter 37

It's a long walk to Adare's school, twice as long as it was from Ennis House, and we have to cross a walking bridge over the highway. Again I let Mom and Adare go ahead of me. I follow behind, watching Adare's red ponytail swing.

We drop Adare off and she stands in a cluster of kids who wait with their special aides to take them to class.

"How are things in your new math class?" Mom asks as we continue on. I still haven't told her about Ms. Alice, her square glasses and her backward teaching.

I keep it in me, closed up like Adare. I think about ripping my shoes off, but instead I say, "I can walk by myself, you know. I do it every day after school."

"I know, but I like our morning walks. Don't you?"

"You didn't care when we took the subway. You didn't always come with us then."

"It would have been another fare."

"So?"

"You know we don't have the money for that."

"Willa did."

She stops. "We are not Willa's responsibility, Cora."

"We could have been."

"No, we couldn't." Then she says, "I think you're right," and for a minute I think she's changing her mind about all of this, our *placement*, our way of living.

Instead, she says, "You're old enough to walk alone. I have to be better about trusting you."

She stops and there's a moment when I do, too. There's a moment when we stand beside each other and think about whether we're really doing what we say.

Then we are. She laughs, ruffles my hair, and says, "We'll meet at the park. I get off early today. I'll try to be there by four o'clock."

So our new placement isn't somewhere we can go after school alone. It's not the safe place she wants it to be. Maybe she sees that I know this because she follows up by saying, "The new place is not like the shelters, Cora. It's more permanent. A big step for us. For all of us."

But I know this is not what home is like, somewhere you can't go on your own.

She kisses my forehead and I swipe it clean, then we walk opposite ways without saying goodbye.

The brownstones are set far back in Carroll Gardens, so the front lawns roll out to the sidewalk. Some of them have religious statues, like women with stone cloaks and men with pointy crowns. The first green is already pushing through. It's the crocuses with their purple smiles sticking up. Next will be the daffodils. Then the tulips in sweet rainbowed rows.

It's the kind of place where people plant things because they know they'll be there to watch them grow.

I stop and loop my arm out from my backpack to get my Tree Book, to write a note that the crocuses have started to come up. I probably should have written it sooner, but I'd been looking too high, waiting for tree buds.

The broken zipper's already undone. There's a trail of my loose papers along the sidewalk. I crouch and grab at each one, darting toward them before the wind picks up. They're worksheets, with my name across the top, and a spiral notebook, in purple, for English.

I hopscotch my way backward, fisting the papers without crumpling them. They're sopped in yesterday's rain. I look over through the gates and stones, making sure nothing blew back. Then I brush the notebook off and stuff everything in, fishing around for my Tree Book.

But it's not there. The worn leather, with its little ribbon tail, is missing. I check the front pocket. I check the sleeve inside. I sit down on the wet ground and throw my backpack to it, opening it wide. I take all the withered papers out and stack them. I take each covered textbook and notebook out. Purple, red, green, blue. I check the front pocket—a jumble of pens and pencils and paper clips, an eraser that feels like it's coated in sand and crumbs. I check the empty sleeve. I fan the colors, in a pinwheel, looking for the soft brown leather.

It's gone.

My heart starts banging and I shove everything inside my backpack, fast. I try to zip it and send myself into a swirling circle, eyeing the sidewalk and the brown grass and the crocuses. I slip my backpack on, tight to my shoulders, and start running.

I run back to where we came from, trying to catch my breath. But it's like I've let all the air go in one giant exhale and I can't get any of it back.

I hear "Hey, Cora!" and look up to see Sabina running after me. "Wrong way!"

I shake my head, words gone from me, caught up in all the lost things.

Chapter 38

"Fresh starts can be good," Sabina says. "Maybe you can get a new book."

We sit against the railing of the walking bridge, listening to the motoring expressway beneath us. It smells like car exhaust and sounds like ocean, with tremors and grumbling every time a tractor-trailer passes underneath.

"It's not just the book. It's . . . everything."

How can I explain it? I want to tell Sabina the truth about things, but I don't want her looking at me the way she did the day she found me in the stairwell.

But then there was that day at lunch, the two of us staring up at the clouds. It might be easier if I didn't have to see her looking at me.

I lean back and look up. The sky's a soft blue now, with the day drying out beneath me.

I take a deep breath and start talking. "Everything's a mess. We left my mom's friend's apartment. We have this placement in Red Hook. It's cold and dark, and there's no light, no nothing. There's no place for me to even set up a greenhouse. There's no way for anything to grow."

I stop and wait for her response. I don't have to see her frowning or shaking her head at me. If I look up, I can only imagine the reaction I want her to have.

And her answer is soft, like she's thinking real hard. "Things can grow anywhere," she tells me. "Look at the canal."

I need her to understand. It's not only about growing things. "You don't know what it's like not to have a place to live. No place has ever been mine."

"I guess. But even if I've been to a million places, I've never really belonged anywhere," she tells me.

I imagine Sabina in her houseboat, how she's never been to a real school until now and doesn't know the real rules for jump the river, how she collects the notes and memories of others, but maybe she's never actually made any lasting memories of her own.

She twirls a braid around her finger. "Sometimes it feels like everyone's got a secret I can't know."

I roll the rubber heels of my sneakers back and forth, my legs sticking straight out. I wonder how she could say exactly what I'm feeling. Maybe it's all the notes and letters and postcards she's been collecting over the years. Or maybe we're both feeling the exact same way.

Then Sabina sighs and I know something's coming. "So, Cora, I mean, I know I'm not exactly experienced with this whole friends thing, but why've you been avoiding me?"

"Avoiding *you*?" I say. "You're the one avoiding *me*."

"*Me*? Why would I do something like that?"

"The other day in the stairwell when I cut class, you looked at me like . . . I don't know. Like I was some *delinquent*."

"*Delinquent*?" She laughs. "Yeah, Cora, you're such a delinquent. With your big old backpack and a notebook clutched at your chest every day."

"Well, why would *I* avoid *you*?"

"Two words. Homeschooled. Freak."

Now it's my turn to laugh. "Sabina, even when you're standing on your head, I like you a gazillion times better than anybody right side up."

She smiles, but then her tone turns serious. "So what's our problem?"

"I don't know. Maybe it's like you said, about not leaving anything behind. Maybe it's easier not to make memories or friends." I swallow hard. "I mean, one of these days one of us is going to leave this place. Then what?"

"I don't know," she tells me.

"Me either."

I don't look at her when I say what I'm about to say next. I look at the clouds, hoping for the best. "Maybe this is a crazy idea, but do you want to find out?"

I don't have to see it to hear it, the smile in Sabina's voice. "Absolutely."

Chapter 39

After Sabina skips off across Hicks Street, waving her hellos at the crossing guard, I keep straight. I walk away from the school, along the metal fence, beneath the subway tracks, past Miss Li, who I can see through the glass sitting at the deli counter with her chin in her hands.

It's March twenty-first and I'm going to the tree. I'm going to get in it and stay there until I know what I'm supposed to know.

I cross the bridge over the canal, looking out over its green ooze, past the abandoned construction, and along the narrow dirt path. It's easier without Adare, like a song on pause, stopping to look up and down or ripping her shoes off. I can walk free and fast.

When I get to the fallen tree, I look for the charcoal cat, but he's not there. I dip to the ground and lay myself along the still-wet dirt. Sabina's notes are tucked on one side. On the other, the screech owl is back, sitting with bunched-up feathers. His eyes are two yellow round moons. He doesn't look scared, even though I feel like he should. Because who am I to him? I'm an Old Lou, sitting and staring and taking up space where I shouldn't be.

I stand up and tiptoe away. The tree's still there, of course. The tall, thin lines of bark stretch up and around, like the in-and-out folds of a skinny accordion.

I walk to the foundry and see the door propped open. I take a deep breath, wondering how on earth I'll convince Anju to let me use her ladder to get to the roof.

But when I step inside, no one's there. Only the giant heart stretching up into the empty dark.

It might be my only chance.

I rush to the ladder and wrap my fingers around one of the steps. Two feet, one hand. Each rung puts me closer to the latched door until I'm at the top rung. I flip the door open wide and yank myself up.

The roof is black and the sun burns bright. I don't look back. I steady myself and walk toward the nearest branch and I'm not even scared, just ready to be inside something, anything, for real.

Gripping the rough bark, my hands feel strong. I sit and bounce up and down, testing my weight. The tree holds me, like I knew it would, because it has to, because there's something about this tree that's Daddy's. I grip hard and swing my legs so I'm on all fours, crawling along the branch like an insect toward the tree's sturdy center.

It's there, at the core, that the tree sprouts out into itself. The branches like petals. The trunk a massive, old, going-nowhere stalk.

I look up. To the heaven Mom sends her love to when she motions the sign of the cross.

I place my foot in an angled nook and wrap my hands around the branch above. Two feet. One hand. Two hands. One foot. I measure it, like this, like climbing the stairs of Ennis House, one flight at a time.

The branches smell grassy and sweet. I don't hear the subway or the cars rumbling on the bridge. It's shaded and cool, and even when I look down at the fallen tree and the canal and the houseboats, I don't feel scared. I feel like I'm somewhere I belong.

I climb as high as I can. I follow the memory of the drawings in my lost book, but there comes a moment when I have to stop and let myself be.

I catch my breath, slam my backpack against the bark, and let my legs dangle on either side of the wide branch.

I look down at the roof and Brooklyn below, trying to see everything I've ever known, every street I've walked. Somewhere, down there, or out there, whether I can see it or not, is every place I've ever lived and every tree I've ever climbed. A real-life map, tucked in one fast, whole vision.

I'm inside Daddy's tree and it feels like now it's not just his. It's ours.

I sit for hours in the memory of the pages of the Tree Book and all the places where I took over Daddy's notes for him. I look at every curve of branch, every new stem, and see the smallest buds sprouting.

I listen to my heart pound in my ears, so loud, so strong, it feels like the only place I can ever make my own.

Then my breath catches, like a snag in a wool coat, and I know what's mine and where I need to be.

With Adare.

Adare will be waiting.

Chapter 40

Adare might not care whether I'm there or not. She probably won't even tell anyone I never came. She'll sit on the school steps. She'll smile and look up at the sky. She'll wait. That's the kind of faith she has in me.

I look at my watch. It's 3:30—twenty minutes *after* I'm supposed to meet her. A half hour *before* we're supposed to be with Mom.

I'm caught in between.

I lean forward, place both hands on the branch, and run the rough bark across my palms, scratching my flesh, knowing I can't leave her even if I wanted to.

It's like she's got me. Adare and her soft-song voice, the way she spins in the rain and follows cats through the dark.

I hold on to the bark, take a deep breath, and climb down. It's slower than going up and I have to be more careful. I secure my feet in every nook and grip one branch at a time until I reach the roof.

But when I get to the hatch, it's shut.

There's no handle and my heart starts ticking like a too-wound clock. I bang at it with a closed fist and call out, "Hey! Anybody in there?"

I wait, with the subway coursing overhead and the bridge thundering every time a car crosses. The canal slinks along into the harbor, which looks so wide and going, going, gone from here. I bang again.

Nothing.

I walk to the edge of the roof and look down, feeling a tingle in my toes as I do. There's no way I can jump. It's too high.

My heart speeds up, but I can't hear it the way I could in the tree. It's just fast and thumping against me like it wants out. Adare will be waiting. She'll wonder where I am or she won't wonder at all. But still, she'll be there. And I won't.

I walk to the hatch. Slam my fists against it again. "Hey! I'm here!" I call. "I'm still here!" I walk back to the edge, look out over the canal, over at Sabina's houseboat. Lifeless. Still.

I'll have to wait until morning, when Anju will come in her smacking boots and wild hair for her heart.

I sit at the edge of the roof. Adare will sit at the steps

like she's always done. Mom will wait at the park like she promised. And I'll be here, with a racing heart, wondering what kind of mess I've made now.

I look up at the sun, which I know will eventually leave the sky.

I don't know what made me think I had any of this figured out.

I set my backpack down and let my head rest on it. The edges of my books poke up into my brain. I cross my arms over my chest and look up at the darkening sky. I haven't eaten anything since breakfast, and no matter how many times I've had to practice being hungry, it never gets easier.

I look below me, realizing I have no choice. I have to find my way down.

Chapter 41

I stand on the lowest branch, at the center of the tree, staring at the ground. I slip my backpack from my shoulders, take a deep breath, and let it go. It doesn't float or waver. It just takes a straight shot to the withered grass.

I decide I'll climb down. I'll hold on to the bark for as long as I can before I let go.

I slide my jacket over my palms, my thumb and fingers jutting out to grip the tree. I hug the trunk, legs and arms wrapped around it, knowing that as soon as I slip, it'll burn and bruise. I only hope that I land flat-footed instead of plain flat.

I'm face to face with the tree. All the jagged lines of bark. Like the cords of a scarf all cabled together.

I take one step at a time.

I know I'll take it slow until I have to be fast. That's how climbing down a tree works. When the slip comes—and it *always* comes—you have to give in and fly.

Just as I think it, I feel a small scrape where my fingers can't grab and I lose everything. My legs go straight and I slide down the tree.

I turn my face, feel the earth pulling at me, think, *Get your feet flat, your hands ready, your hands.* Your hands, Daddy always said, are the best way to fall.

It's fast, the falling. It's one moment you're high and the next you're down. I feel my hands on the matted grass and my feet in a knot, but because I can feel anything at all, I know I'm not dead.

I sit up and catch my breath. I took the tree most of the way down, so I'm scraped instead of broken.

My jeans are sliced and my knee throbs a little. My left hand burns, and when I hold it in front of me, all I see are scratchy, thin lines of flesh and blood and dirt.

My heart drums in my ears and my legs shake, my breath still trying to fill up my chest and let go.

I stand up. There's a moment when I think I'll fall, but I stay steady. I've still got my bulking coat and hanging hair, and my shoes are still attached to my feet.

Then I burst out laughing, the kind of laugh that hurts because of the way it comes up at you, sneaking through your chest and pushing out your throat until it explodes. *I slid down a tree.*

My hand is searing, knife-slice pain, and I catch myself and stop laughing as I remember whose hand I'm supposed to hold.

Chapter 42

I run as best I can with a wobbly knee and my burning hot hand stuffed into my pocket with lint and old tissues.

When I get to the school, looking for Adare at her place on the steps, nothing's the way it should be. Most of the kids are gone and no one's laughing or shouting or talking about who did what where when, and Adare's not staring at the streetlamp or the sky, smiling and wondering and waiting.

The steps are empty.

My heart stings more than my hand, which I stuff deeper into my pocket, clawing at the fabric of my coat. My palm sweats and burns as my chest fills up with all that's gone wrong.

I try not to panic.

Maybe she's in the schoolyard or the office instead. I walk the edge of the building and turn its corner to the wide concrete space with the outline of a basketball court and hoops without nets. It's fenced off and empty and I don't see anybody lingering.

I tell myself it's not like middle school, where people stay for practice or drama club or extra help. She's probably dangling her polka-dot leggings over a seat at the security desk or the principal's office, where kids get sent if nobody's showed up for them.

I pull on the blue doors. There's that drab, mismatching tile I remember. The woman at security has a big puff of silk hair. She grits her gold teeth and asks if she can help me, but she sounds like she doesn't want to deal with me at all.

"I was supposed to pick up my sister," I say. "I'm late."

"Mmm," she says like she doesn't believe me. "Who's your sister?"

"Adare Quinn."

"Oh, Adare!" She breaks into a smile. "She your sister?"

I nod.

"Ain't seen her, but I can check the office."

"Thanks."

She picks up a walkie-talkie. It scratches static as she garbles, "Main office," and I think I hear her say Adare's name.

We wait with the *shhh* stream of the walkie-talkie and she says, "Adare's a breath of sunshine, ain't she?"

I nod, because Adare is a breath of everything, with the way she holds on to it until she can't anymore.

"She's a funny one, but her smile'll break ya, won't it?"

"Yeah," I say softly, like she would, wishing she'd stayed where she was supposed to or, more like, wishing *I* had.

I look through the windowed door into the auditorium, with its rows of seats. It all feels smaller than it did when I was here.

The walkie-talkie smacks a sound back at us and I look to the security guard to translate.

"Nope."

Everything inside me falls like a dumb weight and I feel like I need some of Adare's sunshine breath. This is not good at all.

"You wanna make a call?"

I shake my head real fast.

"Got your own cell?"

I shake my head again. We don't have anyone or anywhere to call, never have. I stand in place, not really sure where to go. I think of how I tried to run away from the day and how, now, it feels like it's running away from me.

The security guard moves her round blue-suited body in her chair, shifts her whole behind, so it squeaks an echo through the empty school. "Somebody's probably come and got her," she tells me. "That's what happens. Somebody got the memo wrong."

I wish she was right. I wish it more than anything. But this is no one's fault but my own.

"Thanks," I tell her. I hold on to the strap of my backpack, push in the sweaty metal bar of the door, and I'm outside on the empty steps, feeling the world—*my* world—get so small, I'm not even sure I fit inside.

Chapter 43

walk to the park without Adare, trying to think of what I'll tell Mom.

Adare wasn't there.

Which isn't true. At all.

I wasn't there.

I've got one hand trapped in my pocket and the other so empty, without Adare, it starts to hurt even more.

Adare has kept all my secrets and I don't even know hers. Where would she go without us? Maybe she's at the park. I'd tell Mom everything if it meant Adare was there.

I pick up my walk, thinking Adare will be at the base of the pin oak, spread out like she's making snow angels in Brooklyn dirt. I find myself running, holding my hand out, so the wind rushes at its red tree burn.

Adare will be there because she has to be.

But when I get there, she isn't.

She's not at the base of the tree and she's not at the bench and she's not at the little stone tables and when I look up into the canopy of trees she's not there, nothing is, just branches and the gaps in between.

Mom is there. She sits on the bench, one leg curled up in her lap, cradling it like a baby.

I stand where I am until she sees me, until she makes her way to me, looking first at my ripped jeans and then at my mangled hand. I say what I wish I didn't have to say. "Adare is gone."

Chapter 44

"So you were late. You were climbing." Mom tries to get the facts, her hands on her hips, ponytail swinging as she paces. "She wasn't in the office. She wasn't in the schoolyard."

I shake my head, my heart leaping hurdles.

"This is a big city, Cora."

"I know."

"Adare is a little girl."

"I know."

"When I tell you to meet Adare, it is not a joke. This is not a joke."

My face is hot. My hand burns. I want her to take it. I want Adare to appear. I want this all to be over. But I can tell it's just begun.

"What's gotten into you?" she asks. "You're keeping

secrets. You're walking away. From Adare. From me. This isn't like you."

I wonder what *is* like me. To follow orders. To be where I'm supposed to be.

"I trusted you."

I'm sorry, I want to say, but the words are caught.

"Do you know what can happen to someone like Adare, alone in this city?"

I shake my head. I don't want to know.

"The worst. *The worst,*" she whispers.

I can tell that this time she has no *next* for us. Everything inside me shakes.

"We'll need to tell the police. How far could she have gone in just one hour?"

I shake my head. I don't know. I don't seem to know anything. "Maybe she's at Ennis House. Or Willa's. Or Miss Li's."

"Miss Li's?"

"The cat," I say.

"What cat?"

"Adare's charcoal cat." But my words get messed up. "Sabina found him."

"Sabina?"

"My friend."

Mom stops pacing. She takes in a breath and her eyes, big and brown, turn glassy as they fill up with tears. I have never seen Mom cry. Not ever. Not even when Daddy died. Not that I saw.

"I'll find her," I say.

She takes my arm. She holds it soft in hers. "You'll stay right here with me."

Chapter 45

The police station is dim and gray like school—the waxy floors and the fluorescent lights with their harsh glow. We sit on plastic chairs.

Officer Torres has pin-straight hair. It's a thick, willowy blond. When she talks, her teeth glow white, and she rolls each *r* like a guitar strum. She speaks softly to us, asks one question right after another about Adare. Address, date of birth, hair, eye color, height, weight, complexion, eyeglasses, braces, body piercings, tattoos. She asks, *Where was she last seen?* School. *What was she wearing?* Polka-dot leggings. A purple wool coat. *Any belongings?* A backpack as blue as the sky.

Officer Torres has a phone that whispers static like the security guard's walkie-talkie. She talks into it. She mentions something about dispatching.

She asks for photos and phone numbers and Mom

shakes her head. She asks for friends and parents of friends and all we can think of is Willa. She asks about custody issues. *My husband is dead.* She asks about grandparents. *None.* She asks if her bedroom has been secured, if she could be hiding in closets or crawl spaces, in piles of laundry, under beds or behind large appliances.

"We haven't . . . It's not—" Mom hesitates.

I say it simple. "We don't have things like that."

She asks what else we have to know about Adare. She says, "Tell me anything. Everything."

I look to Mom, who runs the back of her hand across her eyes. She almost smiles. "Adare is sweet. She lost oxygen to her brain when she was a baby. So she doesn't say much. She smiles a lot. She loves cats. She has this habit of holding her breath. She doesn't like to wear shoes. She doesn't always answer when you ask a question."

"She's always looking up," I say. *Like me,* I think. *But she stays put. Until now.*

Officer Torres looks me over. I see her eyes wander to my torn jeans. She watches me stick my hand in my pocket. "There are no custody issues?" she asks again.

"I told you, my husband is dead."

She nods. "And there's no one who's shown unusual attention or interest in your child?"

Mom shakes her head as I say, "Willa," real fast. Willa wanted us once.

Mom turns to me, stern. "No." Then she tells Officer

Torres, "She doesn't understand what you're asking. Willa is a friend. My friend. And Adare wasn't taken. She wandered off."

"She does this often, then? Wanders?"

Mom's voice is a sudden mouse-quiet. "No."

"She ran off once," I say, and Mom looks at me, confused. "To follow a cat."

"Where?" Officer Torres asks, and I watch Mom look carefully at me for the answer.

"To Miss Li's," I say. And I think of the canal and the tree, the screech owl in the hollowed-out trunk.

"A bodega. In Gowanus," Mom clarifies.

"And you haven't checked your home?"

"We only just moved in."

"Last night," I say. "But she has a good memory. For places."

"Okay. We'll send someone there. And there's no place else you think she could be, except school, the park, Willa's, or this . . . Miss Li's?"

I think of the tree. I had told her it was our secret. Would she go there without me?

"Maybe Ennis House," Mom says. "A shelter. We lived there for a while."

"And Ennis House." She scribbles in her notebook.

My heart bangs fast, thinking of Old Lou on those steps.

Officer Torres nods.

"She's not like other children," Mom explains. "She doesn't have attachment to places or *things*. She likes animals. People."

I say it quiet: "The cat. The tree."

"Yes, in the park," Mom says. "Cora has a favorite climbing tree. That's where she and Adare meet me."

I shake my head. "Not that tree. A different one. I—" I hesitate, thinking of our secret. Daddy's and mine and Adare's. Together. "We have a tree."

Chapter 46

I sit in the back of Officer Torres's car, looking out the window, smelling the musty leather of the seats. My hand's bandaged and stained orange from the iodine and it throbs beneath the sticky white tape.

I watch Officer Torres and Mom through the glass door of Miss Li's. I see how Miss Li turns the volume of her little television down and the way they all stand and nod and shake their heads.

I think of Old Lou creeping on the stairs at Ennis House, his elbows resting on his knees, his wild laugh when I handed him the acorn. What if Adare is there? With him? Adare will hold her breath at the bottom step and maybe she won't set it free.

I breathe more and more air out into the world, hoping it finds a way to her.

Officer Torres climbs into the driver's seat. Mom takes

the other side. The doors slam and I don't even have to ask if Miss Li saw her, from the way they're quiet, their lips flat and straight.

Officer Torres suggests we check the canal and I know I have to tell them where I was when I was supposed to be getting Adare, so I take a breath and tell the truth. "I was just there. Climbing. I didn't see her."

Mom turns, looks at me through the faded glass that separates the back seat from the front. "Shouldn't you have been in school?"

I say nothing, just lift my shoulders into a shrug.

"Well, there's been a lot of time between now and then. Where exactly is it?" Office Torres asks.

I tell her to take the Ninth Street Bridge. We drive slow, looking at every person who passes us. None of them is Adare.

We drive over the bridge and leave the car on the street.

Leading them along the narrow path, I feel like this is our last chance at finding her. My heart beats out a prayer.

We pass the foundry. Mom and Officer Torres walk the high grass, their shoes sticking in the dirt and old leaves.

"*This* is where you've been going?" Mom asks, her hand at her nose, trying not to breathe the stink of the canal.

"Uh-huh." Then I point at the tree.

Their chins lift like they're looking up at a building scraping the sky.

When we reach the dock, it's empty. No charcoal cat.

No Adare. The fallen tree sits alone and I don't see the screech owl inside.

Mom folds her arms and shakes her head and I watch her wipe her eyes, real quick, like she doesn't want anyone to see. Her ponytail has fallen to the side and it leaks wisps of hair she doesn't try to fix.

I look up at the red foundry, thinking how it wasn't long ago I was trying to get down. My head skips visions like a jump-cut video. If I had got down the tree sooner. If I had gone to school. If my backpack had stayed zipped. Maybe everything would be different.

Officer Torres walks the grass, kicking things with her feet, and my eyes have never worked harder to see someone than the way they're working now.

I look at everything. I walk the narrow path, looking at every rock, and then I see, in some overgrown grass, a heap of pink. My mind stops skipping. My heart stops pounding at my ears. I take in all the breath I can.

Adare's high-tops.

"She's here!" I call out.

Even if I can't see her, she has to be. I hear Officer Torres and the static beeps of her phone. Mom rushes to me. I slip to my knees and take the shoes into my hands before Officer Torres tells me, in the rolling hill of her voice, not to touch a thing.

Chapter 47

M om and I use the fallen tree as a bench. Mom sits with forms she's supposed to fill out, but her pen hovers over the pages like a ghost. We sit and wait and I feel the sky edging toward dark. I feel the way the air takes on the cold. Mom doesn't let go of my bandaged hand. For the first time in years, I haven't drawn anything on my palm except the memory of my fall. We hold on to nothing. But we don't let go.

Officer Torres wants us not to move. She thinks Adare's nearby and she wants to end this before dark.

"She wouldn't go far," Mom insists.

"What about the cat? She loves it," I say for my sister. "She'll follow it anywhere."

"They'll find them both," she assures me. "It's their job."

I don't know how you follow the trail of a cat. Or the

trace of a shoeless Adare. "It's my fault," I tell her. "I should have been there."

"No. It's mine."

"I should be with her."

"No, Cora. *I* should be."

I scrape my shoes in the dirt. "Are you going to send Adare to Jade's school?"

"It's the best in the country for kids like her. It's a good opportunity."

"Adare is Adare, like you say. What's the point in figuring her out to be like anyone else?"

"It's not about that. It's about doing what's best for *her*, giving her the best chance. Adare is smart. Smarter than most people give her credit for."

I think of Adare's way with cats and people like Miss Li and the security guard at her school. I think of her pointing out the chimes and the sky and her crows. I always thought it was everyone else seeing past Adare, but maybe it's me.

I point to the houseboat. "My friend Sabina lives there. Her dad's a fisherman."

"That's perfect," she marvels. "A home no matter where you are."

"We could get a houseboat," I say. "You could get a license and we could learn to sail and we could collect rainwater and sun and not have to worry about anything." I look up at her and it feels like a prayer.

She shakes her head, like she's sorry she already let me down.

"It hasn't been fair to you, living like we do. I know that. But I'm trying to make sense of where we are. Where we need to be. And *you*, you try harder than anyone I know. I love a lot of things about you, but that's one of the things I love best."

She takes her hand from mine and looks down at the forms. She clutches her pen and writes in the date. March twenty-first.

The day Daddy and his notes disappeared. Then my Tree Book. Now Adare.

"My Tree Book's gone," I tell her.

"Gone?" She looks almost as sad as I do. "Where could it have gone?"

"It's lost."

"Maybe it was only on loan," she says. "Maybe it's back where it belongs." She looks up to the branches of the tree and I look up with her.

"That's the tree of heaven."

"No way." She shakes her head, like she doesn't believe me. "Your father's?"

"This is it. This is the one." I watch her stare up into its branches. "I climbed it," I tell her. "I could hear my heartbeat. I could see everyth—"

I don't even finish the words.

Of course. The tree.

I'll be able to see anything from there.

Before I know what I'm doing, I'm off, running toward the foundry to get up it as fast as I can.

The door is closed, but I bang at it, hoping someone will hear.

"Cora!" I hear Mom call out.

I look around in a fever, a whirl, like Adare's spinning rain dance. There's a heap of scrap metal, broken stone, brick, and piles of lumber. I take a heavy brick in my hand. I back up and then I take off running forward, hurling the brick at the knob, shaking the knob loose, so it swivels in a loop-the-loop.

I shake the knob, fiddling with the metal, pushing at the lock until the door swings open and in.

The last of the daylight fills up the gray room. I run past the giant heart, straight for the far wall, toward the ladder.

Then I hear a mewing cat.

I snap my gaze back to the misshapen heart and see the charcoal cat in a curl. He rests against two little bare feet.

Adare.

I collapse into her for a hug, but she squirms from me, kicking her feet and giggling.

"What are you doing *here?*" I ask through a smile so big I almost can't manage it.

Her eyes shine in the dark.

"Looking," she tells me.

"Here?"

"For you."

Like Anju said, *el corazón*. I look up at the hard metal lines of the brassy pink.

Mom crosses through the light from the door and crouches down beside us, grabbing Adare and cradling her in her arms. "We were so worried," she tells her. "We love you so much."

Adare nestles her head in Mom's chest.

"How did you get in?" I ask.

"Anju." She shrugs and pulls the cat into her arms.

"But the door."

"Yeah." And she doesn't say much more than that. The charcoal cat slinks around, nudges his chin at Adare's side.

"He doesn't belong here," I say. "He belongs wherever you are. Don't you think?"

Adare nods. "I love him."

I say, "I know."

I look over to the ladder on the wall and the hatch above. I think of the lost notebook, the tree of heaven, and all the things that sent us here to this moment.

March twenty-first.

Chapter 48

It takes time to figure out the sounds of a place. Some places have footsteps cracking the floors, a rattle in the stairwell, or the creak of an elevator shaft. There could be highway hum or rustling trees, lights buzzing in the hallway.

Tonight, here in our *placement,* it's quiet. The walls are thick. Sometimes I hear a door slam, but the sound disappears. I lie in the dark next to Adare. I match up our palms. I let our toes touch. I listen to the best sound: her breath next to mine.

I close my eyes.

I think of her sitting inside the heart, the word meaning me, *el corazón.* I think of Officer Torres writing up her report with a smile at her lips. I think of Anju explaining how she let Adare in, told her to close the door behind her, which Adare took to mean to close the door then. I think how Officer Torres drove us home in the police car and dropped us off in front of our brick building and asked, "Is this you?"

I think how a place could be a home, could be yours, could be *you*.

I think how we answered. *Yes.*

Then I drift into sleep, feeling Adare shifting next to me, and the rhythm of her breath. I feel a release.

I sit up fast, panicking in my tank top and underwear, shuffling my legs. *Not again. No. Not again.*

But I'm not sitting in a wet puddle—I'm pressing on the air mattress, sinking to the floor, while the air lets out in a slow, whistling ooze. Adare rustles, moans. Mom says from her beanbag cushion, "What's that?"

"The mattress," I say in the dark.

Mom moves, slow, to the light switch. The bulb bursts on above us and we're rubbing our eyes, trying to go from dark to light, and Adare's awake and yawning and whimpering in her butterfly wings because it hurts her eyes and Mom is shushing while we feel around for the poking hole, for the air escaping.

"Stand up," Mom insists, and I take Adare's hand, lift us both above the flopping mat. "Get the Band-Aids."

I leave Adare and turn on a blast of yellow light in the bathroom. I take out the Snoopy Band-Aids from the medicine chest and bring them to Mom.

"It's punctured," she says with a sigh. "How could

that—" she starts, but stops, shaking her head. I can see it makes her mad, but she's trying to pretend it's fine.

I stand with Adare crouched at my feet. She's whining without words, like she isn't really awake.

Mom sits back on her hands. "Well, I think I got it," she says. "But we should figure out what made this hole." She starts searching around the mattress.

I don't know what it could be. We don't have much here in the first place.

I scoot down to the floor, running my fingers over the hard wood. Adare curls up like she's going to fall asleep.

Her wings are strapped to her back, all old and worn. Then I see what must have done it. There's a wire poking out from one wing's sparkled edge. I'm about to point and tell Mom what's going on when I stop.

I don't want Mom taking away Adare's wings.

I've got to figure out something else.

I see my backpack slumped on the floor and I feel around it, pretending I'm searching, just like Mom. I slip my hands into the outer pocket and pull out a pen.

I hold it up. "This must've done it," I say. "I was drawing before bed."

Mom swings around, takes the pen from me, and I don't know what I'm expecting, what she really can say about it, whether it even matters if it's a pen or a tack or Adare's old butterfly wings, but if she's got anything to get mad about, she might as well get mad at me. "Well . . ."

She places a hand at her hip. "We'll need to be more careful. Until we get a real mattress."

And that's all.

"Can you put the Band-Aids away?"

I nod, fast. Then I take Adare's hand. "Adare, come help me," I say. "I need your help putting the Snoopys away. Okay?"

"Okay." She stands up like the world's going to end and drags herself to the bathroom with me while Mom places the pen on the kitchen counter and moves across the room to shut off the light.

I set Adare on the toilet seat. She doesn't know what she's done and it doesn't matter, really, but I bring my finger to my lips anyway, like it's our secret to share.

I start unpeeling the backings from Snoopy Band-Aids. They're like sticky little ribbons and I loop them around and around the wire to fix the broken wings.

Chapter 49

We walk from Adare's school alone for the first time back to Red Hook. We've each got a ribbon on our wrists with a little silver key dangling. When Mom wound the purple ribbon around Adare's wrist this morning, Adare held it up, and it sparkled across her eyes.

Mom said she'd talk to her boss about getting her hours switched so they matched ours. Then she looped the satin around the bump of my wrist and told me not to worry, promised she'd be the one to keep us safe.

She made me make two promises, too. "Don't keep so many secrets."

"I won't. I swear. What's the second?" I asked. *No climbing*, I thought.

Instead, she smiled. "Climb high."

This time when Adare stops, I stop with her. When

she points, I lift my gaze. I'm not the one dragging Adare through this world. She's the one leading me.

"Hey, Cora!" Sabina calls to us from the corner, with her schoolbooks pancake-flattened beneath her arm.

I wave and run toward her. "Hey!"

"So I have this idea. About making a book."

"Okay."

"A memory book."

"With all the notes you find?"

"No," she says. "Like my own book, with my own memories."

"So a diary?" I ask.

"Well, it's not as romantic when you put it that way. A *memory book*," she corrects me.

"Just don't lose it," I tell her.

"That's the thing. I know it's not the same as your Tree Book, but I thought we could share it. We can read what the other person says and remember it for each other. That way, if one of us has to leave, we won't forget what happened. What do you think?"

I hesitate. I don't know about starting a new book. But then I wonder what it would be like to share a book with someone who's here in my life, now. "Okay." I start nodding. "Yeah."

"Awesome. So I'll see you tomorrow?"

I nod. "Tomorrow."

She smiles and squeaks her heel, taking off toward the canal. Adare waves, even though Sabina is long gone.

We cross the walking bridge into Red Hook, passing the church steeple and the highway. When we reach the brick building and our bright blue apartment door, I walk up close and run my fingers across the faded number of our place. I trace it. A number 7 and an *A* are smacked together. The answer to Ms. Alice's equation.

7A. *Found.*

I stand in front of the door. *Our* door. Not like at Ennis House, where all we had was a door that could have been anybody's.

I take a whiff of all the cooking smells and I imagine *frijoles charros* mixed up in them.

I let Adare turn the key and open the door to the empty apartment. Our things still sit hunched in the corner. There's the air mattress with the Snoopy Band-Aids. Sookie skulks over to Adare and the charcoal cat follows. We decided yesterday to let him be ours.

I sink to the floor with Adare as she strokes their chins. I look around, watching a crack of falling sun slip through the alley and in through the window. "What do you think?" I ask.

Adare giggles. "Big," she says.

She's right. It's bigger than any other place we've been. I wonder how we'll fill it.

The sun catches a hint of something on the ledge. I stand up, wander to the window, and lift the latch.

"Adare—look." I take the silver button and hold it out to her. Is it possible they've found us?

She runs past my outstretched hand to the window and points. I whip my head around to watch a black crow smudging across the alley, taking off into the sky.

Then I hear footsteps and a key turn as the doorknob twists. Mom looks relieved to see us here. But she also looks like she knew we would be.

"What do you think?" Mom echoes as she lets a brown grocery bag slide to the floor. She tousles Adare's hair. We sit together, all three of us on the bare floor, in a perfect linked chain.

I close my eyes and say what I see. "There's an African violet on the sill. And the ceiling's blue, like sky. My greenhouse is an old aquarium, and when the stems and leaves are sturdy enough, we transfer it outside so everyone can see what we grew. We've got a round table with four chairs. Three for us. And one for Willa. And when people come over, they can't believe how much it smells like cinnamon."

I open my eyes and watch Mom open hers, like she's been dreaming it, too. "I like that. What about you, Adare? Do you?"

"Yeah," she says.

"And one more thing," I say.

"What?" Mom asks.

"A set of chimes."

Mom takes my hand. I take Adare's hand with my other, and it's funny how her weird grip has started to feel right.

"What do we have today?" Mom whispers.

I haven't drawn anything in my palm. Not since we came here. And even though it's blank, or *because* it is, I say, "Everything."

ACKNOWLEDGMENTS

Thank you to my agent, Rebecca Stead, for believing in this book. I feel so lucky to have you by my side on this journey. Allison Wortche, the excitement, love, and care you have for Cora and her story has meant so much to me. Thank you both for making my dream of publishing a book come true.

Julia Maguire, Jenny Brown, Melanie Nolan, Karen Greenberg, Marisa DiNovis, and the rest of the Knopf team, I am grateful this novel is in such capable, smart, and caring hands. Thank you also to Michelle Andelman for your enthusiasm for my work.

I would not have come this far in my writing life without the support of many talented writers who are also amazing friends. Thank you to the earliest readers of Cora's story: Janet Sumner Johnson and Alison Cherry. Your thoughtful feedback was invaluable. Tracy Weiss, thanks for bottomless glasses of wine and the endless reading you have done for me. Heather Leah Huddleston, I am grateful for your careful reads, chats, and laughter. Beth Kephart, thank you for reading, listening, and for your love and encouragement over the years. You believed in me long before I knew how to believe in myself. Sharon Mayhew, Amy Sonnichsen, Jennifer Chen, Dianne Salerni, Lauren Gibaldi, and Phoebe North, I couldn't ask for better partners and friends in this writing life. It is because of you that sitting alone with words is never lonely.

Thanks to Carmen Colon for your careful read of an early draft. Thanks also to Jessica Palmer and Patricia Romano for answering my questions about your families and backgrounds. Rebecca Fishman and Shilpa Londhe, I am grateful to you for holding me accountable and for inspiring me with the incredible work you do. Lynn Monaghan, the query whisperer, "thank you for being a friend."

Thank you to all the wonderful educators and administrators at Variety Child Learning Center. My experiences there helped inform Cora and Adare's story. A special thank you to Dr. Fern Sandler for helping me better understand Adare.

Taryn Cunha, Nastasia Sidarta, and the Gowanus Canal Conservancy, I appreciate you answering my questions about plant life around Brooklyn and the canal.

I am grateful to all my family for your love and faith. Mom and Dad, thank you for being my biggest cheerleaders. Your love guides me every day. Rosemary, my first stories were born at your kitchen table. Grandma Angie, I'll never forget your love of books and the stack at your bedside table. Grandma Kitty, stories about you have long stirred my imagination and wonder.

Finally, thank you to Tyler, who inspired the confidence I needed to find my voice. You keep me rooted in love and optimism, always. Owen, you shared the earliest days of your life with the seeds of this story and helped me see it through. I was only able to write it because my heart was so full.